RED SEASON

GARY GENARD

Cedar &
Maitland
Press

Red Season is a work of fiction. People, places, organizations, and events portrayed are either products of the author's imagination or are used fictitiously.

Copyright 2023 by Gary Genard

All rights reserved. No part of this book may be reproduced in any form without written permission from the publisher, except for brief quotations in critical articles or reviews. For information, please contact Cedar & Maitland Press, 23 Robbins Road, Arlington, MA 02476.

First Edition

Cover design: Llywellyn

Interior typesetting: Lorna Reid

ISBN: 978-1-7365556-4-4

Library of Congress Control Number: 2024901636

Printed in the United States of America

To order this book, please call (617) 993-3410 in the U.S., or contact info@garygenard.com. Group discounts are available.

Visit the author's website at www.garygenard.com

In memory of Robert J. Marland

Her lips were red, her looks were free,
Her locks were yellow as gold:
Her skin was white as leprosy,
The nightmare Life-in-Death was she,
Who thicks man's blood with cold.

Samuel Taylor Coleridge, *The Rime of the Ancient Mariner*

CAST OF CHARACTERS

William Scarlet, M.D. — Physician, police surgeon and occult investigator.

Django Pierce-Jones — Secretary of The Society, a medium.

Ambrose Reed — A young artist on his way up, a widower.

Mary Boyle Reed — His wife, now three years deceased.

Elizabeth Wilson — Ambrose's ex-fiancée.

Mrs. Morana Bain — A mysterious lady. Does she ever smile?

Horace Bilby — "The Reader." A man who reads a great deal.

Sir Edward Mallinson, M.D. — Chief Surgeon of the Metropolitan Police (Scotland Yard).

Det. Sgt. James Jessey — A serious and capable policeman with a secret.

Hiram Wilson — Elizabeth's father. Head of the Railway Department.

Margaret Wilson — Elizabeth's mother. Tends to fade into any wallpaper present, but it is an illusion.

Catherine Wilson — Elizabeth's older sister. Beautiful and smart, unmarried.

Thomas Geach — A snake-like man who wears dark glasses at night.

MEMBERS OF THE SOCIETY FOR SUPERNATURAL AND PSYCHIC RESEARCH

Sir Hugh Rodney — A famous architect.

Thaddeus ("Teddy") Locke — A banker with lips as tight as his loans.

Adolphus ("Dolly") Addams — An aristocrat and horse breeder.

Joseph Trippel III — A young man who sees the humour in his own name.

James Scorgie — Ungentlemanly owner of *The Daily Post* newspaper.

Julius Pickering — Founder of the Pickering Grocers chain.

Charles Cobb, Lord Nesbit — A wise old counselor.

John Borland,
Sixth Earl of Caversham — A privileged rising Member of Parliament.

Jacob Blum — A successful and arrogant shipbuilder.

Enzo Conti — Vintner of renowned wines from Italy.

Holman Fisher, Junior — A young chap who is ready for anything.

Coroner, murderers, corpses, dissectors, policemen, devotees of séances, servants, and city dwellers.

Scene: London, 1887.

PROLOGUE

12 November 1863, 8.34 p.m.

t felt as though Father had brought in a paving stone from the street outside and struck him in the forehead with it. He had never felt pain in his head like this, though as soon as Father stopped touching him on the shoulder, the pain vanished. In its place a deep silence arose, which somehow became a sensation of fog—as though the fog was a manifestation of the silence.

To Will Scarlet's nine-year-old mind the sensations were strange and mysterious, even more so than his father attending him at bedtime like this. To the boy, James Scarlet was ever a monument somewhere in the distance: a huge and shadowy edifice that no one or anything would ever move. He was the famous alienist (Father preferred the term 'psychiatric doctor') at St John and St Elizabeth Hospital, a two-minute walk from their home on Grove End Road in the St John's Wood section of London. His was a life of respectability and Olympian heights (Will knew what that meant): the honours, the receptions, the famous cases, and for Will, glimpses of his parents in evening dress and forever saying goodnight.

"All right, my boy?" Dr. Scarlet asked now.

"Yes, Father."

"Not daydreaming, are you?"

"No, Father."

Dr. Scarlet patted his shoulder again—and BAM!, the invisible hammer hit Will a second time. This time a scene opened in his mind, and he was *there*, in that place and time.

Can't see a thing in this fog. Cold here. Shouldn't the air be warm and the ground cold if there's fog? You're on a bridge, you fool, and it's the Thames underneath you, not the ground. No wonder you're cold. Listen. That's the sound of water lapping and the boats' engines, and the hulls slapping down into the boats' wake.

Here's a breeze, and the fog is thinning. There he is—ahead of me on the walkway, moving at a steady pace. No wonder, for he isn't old. Pick up my own pace, try to keep the same distance. My God, he's barefoot. Nothing on but a thin, dirty white shirt, and old trousers frayed at the bottom. He's stopping, and turning around. He sees me—he's looking right at me. I'll stop without going any closer.

He shaved today; I wouldn't have expected it. Can't miss that prominent nose. He's not smiling, so I can't see the crooked brown teeth. Looking at me with those deep-set eyes in that perfect oval of a face. Odd—his hair is neatly combed, too. You'd think he wouldn't have taken the time for that. Such a thick head of hair, not moving at all though there's a stiff breeze out here. Standing still, looking at me without any expression, just blinking slowly. There's recognition there— yes, I'm sure of it. But nothing else. As though every other thought or feeling has departed.

He's shivering. Now he's turning around, and starting off again.
KEEP GOING. GET OFF THE BRIDGE.
As though he can hear my thoughts! Wait. He's stopped again. Crossing to the railing. Standing there with his hand on the stonework.
DON'T.
Walk faster . . . it doesn't matter now if he knows what I'm doing.
He's climbing onto the railing. Go—run to him. He's straightening up . . . leaning over.
NO!
There's the splash. Where is he? I can't see him. Is his head bobbing somewhere? It would be so small and hard to see. No, nothing, just the

black water. I don't even know where to look, as I can't tell how fast the current is carrying him.

Heaven help us . . . the poor man. Should I call for help, run for a policeman?

Why? I know he let himself go under.

Suddenly, Will was back in bed, and staring up at his father. Had Father seen his reactions to the strange vision? There was no expression in James Scarlet's eyes. How long had it all taken? It was hard to tell, as Father's face never gave anything away.

Surely, monuments only noticed big things like other monuments, not boys' reactions. Father said something, but Will didn't catch what it was; it was almost as though he was still hearing the wind on the bridge. Probably, "Time to go to sleep, son." He nodded. That would be a safe reaction to whatever Father had actually said.

How mysterious it all was. He would consider what it meant tomorrow—what he thought had happened, and why it had taken place. He might mention it to Mother, but he thought he probably wouldn't.

For now, he was tired. His lids closed and he was no longer seeing through his father's eyes and thinking his father's thoughts, as he had on the bridge.

CHAPTER 1

The Madness of Crowds

It was the Queen's Golden Jubilee, and the country was quite mad with it.

Yesterday, the 20th of June, had come around again for the fiftieth time since the morning in 1837 when an eighteen-year-old girl was awakened at Kensington Palace. Alexandrina Victoria was told immediately that she was now Queen of England and the United Kingdom, Empress of India, Queen of Canada, Australia, and New Zealand, and Head of the Commonwealth. Now, in 1887, Victoria was 68 years old. Over these two days—for the first time since her beloved husband, Albert, Prince Consort had died in 1861 of typhoid fever—the Queen was appearing in public.

In honour of the Jubilee, the windows, roofs, and bridges of London had sprouted people. A great banquet had been held on the first day of the celebration at Buckingham Palace, which 50 European kings and princes attended. Today—at this very moment!—a magnificent procession was making its way along the Mall to Trafalgar Square. From there, it would visit Westminster Abbey, where a Thanksgiving service was to be held. The Queen was seated in a gilded landau drawn by six Creams. In front of the carriage rode twelve Indian officers, and in front of them, Victoria's three surviving sons, five sons-in-law, nine grandsons and grandsons-in-law. Then came the carriages containing three of her daughters.

In Trafalgar Square, the procession approached a red-and-gold banner strung up on poles on either side of the road which read:

THE LORD BLESS AND KEEP THEE. THE LORD MAKE HIS FACE TO SHINE UPON THEE.

At the moment the Queen's carriage passed under the banner, the forty-four-year-old abbess of a disorderly house known as Mrs. Honey was being slowly strangled with the collar of her dress in a room on Kemble Street, less than a mile away.

"God Save the Queen!" a man whom the landau had just passed shouted.

And the crowd roared its approval.

Dr. William Scarlet had spent the previous evening at his club, the Athenaeum, before returning home early. He was making a concentrated effort to avoid all things Jubilee. His home in the borough of Chelsea was far enough from the Palace that he could do so—provided you avoided the traffic on the Fulham Road and Brompton Road in one direction, and the Kings Road and Eaton Square in the other.

Dr. Scarlet was thirty-three years old, the only child of James and Cordelia Scarlet, and like his now-deceased father, a physician. He lived at One, Beaufort Circle, Chelsea, in a comfortable Georgian home with his cats Marigold and Hercules and two servants: his man Jeffries and Mrs. Bennie, his cook/housekeeper. As his personal wealth was secure, he maintained only a small private surgery in his home, and a house physician appointment at St George's Hospital, where he had attended medical school. Much more of his time was taken up with his duties as an Assistant Chief Surgeon with the Metropolitan Police, commonly known as Scotland Yard.

He stood a half-inch under the six-foot mark, was slim of build and gave the overall impression of a younger man. That impression was misleading, however, for he was well-muscled, and when necessary could move with strength and determination. He appeared calm and placid when thinking; but this too was an erroneous impression, for though he thought calmly, he did not do so placidly. His mind was fast, and when he had decided on a thing, he acted quickly. His appearance was further marked by a wide reddish streak on the front left side of his otherwise light-brown hair, and an even more vividly red, bushy mustache. People often remarked (to themselves) that his mustache was the perfect justification for his name, or vice versa.

This morning, he had the feeling that he would not be able to repeat yesterday's feat of remaining relatively invisible on the second day of the two-day Jubilee, and he was right. He was just leaving his surgery when he was brought to ground by the intrepid Sgt. Jessey of B Division. Clearly, the jig was up.

"I'm sorry to spoil your holiday, sir," said the Sergeant when Scarlet, having locked the door at the side entrance to his surgery, turned around and nearly walked into him. Apparently, he had been just about to pull the bell knob.

The physician knew Jessey to be a family man, and if anyone was being deprived of the madness of crowds today, surely it was the Sergeant and his family. But, as always, Jessey's mouth was set with characteristic resolve concerning the task at hand. There was nothing else for it, Scarlet knew.

"Quite all right, Sergeant. What do you have?"

"I've a murder, sir. At least I'm thinking I have. And I could use your help."

"You mean to certify the death?" the doctor asked.

"Not quite, sir. To locate the victim."

"I'm afraid I don't understand."

Jessey's usual matter-of-fact manner took over. "It's Mrs. Honey, sir, the madam of the house on Kemble Street, up that way. She's disappeared, and I've detained Timothy Macready on the matter. Well, he's her bully, you know." The Sergeant tipped forward stiffly from the waist, as though the next remark was confidential. "I always knew she was in for it someday from him, and now it's happened. I just haven't been able to get it out of him yet."

"I see. If I follow you, Sergeant, you have a disappearance on your hands that you believe is murder. And you have a suspect that you've detained and have been questioning. Though I take it he's been uncooperative?"

Jessey nodded briskly. "That's it exactly, Mr. Scarlet."

"Where is he now, this Macready?"

"I paid a visit to his room, sir—he has a ramshackle type of place in the Strand Underpass, 'round the corner from Kemble Street." The Sergeant allowed himself a grin. "If I'm not mistaken, he's waiting for us there."

"I'll bet he is," said Scarlet, as he followed Sgt. Jessey to the curb.

The cab which the Sergeant had waiting took some time to negotiate the crowded thoroughfares between Scarlet's surgery at Beaufort Circle and the area around Drury Lane. Macready's living quarters were on the second floor of a rooming house that seemed to remain standing only by the will of God. The two men climbed the staircase that even in the light of morning was dark and dismal, smelling of fish. They entered a two-room arrangement with filthy walls that contained barely the necessities, provided you used the word liberally. Macready himself sat on the bed in the inner room of the two, shackled to the bed frame by his thick right wrist. A uniformed policeman stood between him and the doorway to the kitchen.

Scarlet's gaze went immediately to the laceration and ecchymosis above the man's left eye. If such a fresh cut and bruising could somehow suit a face, it did for this man. This one was a brute, and no mistake. Macready was heavy of face and build. But Scarlet had no doubt he'd have sprung at any of them with deceptive speed, had the irons not been in place. He was dull of expression, slack-jawed, though his eyes watched each of them cunningly. Where his gaze came to rest, the eyes narrowed slightly, as though he were defying whoever or whatever he was looking at. He was of the average height, narrow in the shoulders but thick in the arms, with hands that testified to his trade of keeping 'his ladies' in line. There was something simian and challenging and servile, all at the same time, in his manner.

Sergeant Jessey had apparently decided to assume the role of host. "Mr. Macready is helping with our enquiries, Doctor, concerning the disappearance of a certain landlady of the neighborhood."

Macready's eyes shifted immediately to the new visitor. "This one's a doctor, is it? Better at cutting me throat?" He laughed, a dry, unpleasant grating sound as though his throat were filled with gravel.

Scarlet removed his hat—today as usual it was a charcoal grey John Bull top hat without a ribbon above the brim—and looked at Macready steadily, getting the lay of the land. Sgt. Jessey had no authority to detain the man in his own lodgings like this, of course. Not only did no evidence of criminal behavior exist, but there was as yet no proof of a crime in the first place—never mind a coroner's findings on the nature of a death and referral of the prisoner to the courts, necessary steps in every case. No interrogation should be taking place at all.

On the other hand, there was no doubt that Jessey knew his bailiwick inside and out: the people, the shops, and the goings-on. The Sergeant would be aware of events that had taken place that weren't generally known about, as well as things that were likely to happen and worth keeping an eye out for. Evidently, he had been of a mind that this woman—or another of Macready's ladies—might disappear at some point. Perhaps one or another already had before now. As to whether these proceedings were quite as they should be, Scarlet knew that whatever happened in these rooms, Jessey would say nothing of his involvement if Jessey's own actions were discovered.

It would also be just like the Sergeant to have administered this laceration and bruising to provide the necessary pretext for a police surgeon to be here. He wasted no time now using Jessey's subterfuge to his own advantage.

His features abruptly assumed an angry expression.

"Sergeant, what have you been doing to this man?"

"Beg pardon, sir," replied Jessey evenly. "As I said, he's helping with our enquiries."

"Which means, I take it, that you beat him until he says what you want him to?"

Macready's gaze went back and forth during this spirited exchange, watching each man closely as he spoke.

Without waiting for any further reply from Jessey, Scarlet placed his hat on the nearby scarred bureau and walked briskly to the bedside. "Here," he said, "let me look at you." And placing his hand under Macready's chin, he lifted the man's head to catch the light from the window.

But at the touch, the man, the bed, the room, and everything else disappeared. Scarlet immediately felt the familiar blow-like shock which rocked his head back slightly.

She's terrified, the fat ugly cow. I ain't never seen her this close, her face only inches from my own. Look at her eyes, bulging with surprise, her mouth open like a fish's. Can't breathe, Dearie? Ye can't, can ye? My hands is too strong! I've got the collar of yer dress tight in my grip. Tight, tight, like THIS. *God! There's a sight. Her face is turning dark red, now purple.* HERE, *a little tighter. No blood can get back to yer heart, can it, love? And look at the eyes: getting dull, uninterested-like. Looking sleepy now. . . . That's it. Whatever was in them just went out. I can let go of the bitch now. Oooh, she dropped just like a sack of . . .*

Flour.

Well, THAT*'s an idea, and a good 'un! Pearson's is near here, too. A wheelbarrow will do to get her there.*

'Cor, she's heavy to drag, this one. The flour on the floor makes her

slide a little easier, though. Crikey, it's everywhere, covering everything, and in the air, too. Well, what d'you expect in a flour wholesaler? Tickling me nose too. 'choo! 'choo! 'choo! Sneezin' me bleedin' head off! Ugh, she's a bloody cow, this one, and no mistake. I'm puffing like a fucking steam engine. Okay, here's a good spot, let her go. Oi! Her head hit the floorboards with a right smack, didn't it? Ha! Ha! Doesn't matter now, does it, Dearie?

This shipping platform is perfect, with all them barrels. Christ, I'm strong!—this barrel's full and I can still roll it out. Pry this lid off . . . there. Now, tip 'er over. That's too slow, better use my hands too. 'Cor, it's a right avalanche of flour, looks just like snow.

All right, the barrel's empty enough now, she'll fit. Leave some flour at the bottom, though, to deaden the sound. In you go, love, head first . . . have yourself some nice pastry, now. Ha! Ha! Good, there's a shovel they must use to fill the barrels. Well, I will, too, covering her up! I'll scoop up the rest now with my hands. There. The floor doesn't look very different, with this fucking flour everywhere.

Here's a mallet . . . bang the lid shut. Now, roll it back into place with the others. Oof! A barrel with an old whore in it is heavier than a barrel of flour! I'll set up me own bake shop: 'Old Whore Pastries.' Our goods is a bit heavier than our competitors, but we satisfies more! Okay, it's back in place with the others.

Go over here, take a look back at them barrels. . . . Lovely! I can't tell which one she's in. I'd like to see the face of the baker who opens up that barrel in his shop! By that time, I'll be long gone, over to Scutter's place in Gravesend.

Hoy—well done, mate. Next time, I'll sell one for pork pies. And after that, I'll melt one down for candles. I'll have three new professions: I'll be a butcher, a baker, and a candlestick maker!

Scarlet let go of the man's chin. He looked into Macready's eyes. He saw curiosity, suspicion, confusion. But not comprehension. How could the murderer have known what Scarlet was seeing, after all? He'd leave it at that.

"Be sure to wash that cut," he said evenly. "And if you can get hold of some ice, apply it to your forehead. It's nothing serious." He realized that Macready, almost certainly as familiar with receiving as well as doling out punishment, would already know that.

He collected his hat, then turned to Jessey. "As for you, Sergeant," he said severely, "consider this a warning. If I see any more evidence of prisoner abuse like this, your division commander will hear about it. Am I clear?"

"Perfectly, sir."

"Now if you'll see me out, I'll attend to my other duties. And Sergeant, I advise you to arrest this man or let him go. This isn't a boxing exposition."

He nodded curtly to the uniformed policeman, and led the way out of the rooms and down the stairs.

When he and Jessey were safely out of the building, he turned to the sergeant.

"Too thick?"

Jessey smiled. "I don't think so, sir. He'll know your chastisement of me meant nothing and was all for show. And, indeed, it was, wasn't it?"

Scarlet nodded, but his expression was serious.

"Do you know of any baking concern in the neighborhood, Sergeant? Some place that does a large volume of business, perhaps with more than one shop?"

"There's Pearson's Baking Goods Supply on Kean Street. It's a wholesaler's for bakers, though, not a bakery."

"Well, wherever it is, there will be a loading platform with a number of barrels filled with flour. I'm afraid the poor woman's body is stashed in one of them. What I saw was at night, so I'm guessing he took her there late last night or in the early hours of this morning. The barrel is probably still there, or we'd have heard about it by now if it was delivered and opened."

"The bloody bastard. I'll find her, I will. And I'll know from that bully how and why he did it, never you fear, Mr. Scarlet."

Scarlet didn't fear it, and believed Jessey.

"I'll be at home when you know more," he said, and turned away.

It was a wicked world in which one had to hope, as he did now, that people wouldn't begin telling jokes about dead women in pies.

He decided to walk from the rooming house to his home in Chelsea rather than taking a cab. He wanted the time to think and to clear his head.

The strange power that had been at work in Macready's filthy tenement just now was as much a mystery to him as when it first manifested itself, that night when he was nine and his father had tucked him into bed. It came when he had established touch with someone, or when he handled something that that person had touched—any object, as mundane as a sheet of paper or as personal as an item of clothing. The visions, in which he saw through that person's eyes and thoughts, always arrived without warning, and he could never predict when they would come. The entire phenomenon seemed as removed as possible from his life as a scientist and physician. Yet it was as much a part of who he was as those more rational pursuits.

The ability to see and participate in others' experiences—past and future—through objects and touch. The name for it was *psychometry*. A strange gift. Or was it a curse?

The sun this morning seemed to bring out the colors in everything around him as he walked, so unlike the usual gray world of the London streets. It was at times like this that his mind seemed strange and unpredictable to him: a house whose bright rooms could lead to secret shadowy places between one step and the next.

The first time he'd experienced his ability—his vision of the man on the bridge—it had been his father's touch that had taken him into James Scarlet's mind. In an instant his bedroom had simply disappeared, and he was in another time and place. The sights, sounds, and sensations were complete—as though he were actually there experiencing what his father had gone through. Later, when the shock was over, he realized that he'd known other things concerning that moment in time. The man had been a patient at St John and St Elizabeth's Hospital where his father practiced, a depressive who had committed suicide some months earlier by drowning himself in the Thames. The elder Dr. Scarlet had been out that night looking for the man, had found him and had witnessed the tragedy. Those few moments on the Battersea Bridge that James Scarlet had lived through were what Will had experienced when his father had touched him. Why his ability had announced itself when he was that age was also a mystery to him.

Psychometry.

It had happened many times since then, and always completely unexpectedly. The visions he saw weren't necessarily related to important events in the lives of the people he touched or who touched him—he was just as likely to experience ordinary moments as eventful ones. Many times, the situation he found himself experiencing was simply inexplicable to him. And even though he was sure that some of the events he was witnessing hadn't happened yet, he never had the feeling that he could *prevent* them from taking place. At any rate, he had learned how to conceal his response when the visions hit him. It would be madness for him—a physician and police surgeon—to reveal the truth, and so only a handful of people knew his secret.

Sgt. Jessey was one of those people. He had not chosen to tell the man his secret; but sometime over the past few years in their work together, Jessey had guessed the truth. Though Scarlet often felt cursed with his ability, today was one of those times when he realized that it could be a blessing. A vicious killer would mount the gallows because of what he'd seen in the man's mind.

As to the rest of it—the story Jessey would come up with about how he'd uncovered the murder and Scarlet's role—if any—that was the sergeant's business. For now, he'd enjoy this glorious morning that was revealing itself as he made his way homeward.

CHAPTER 2

The Society for Supernatural and Psychic Research

"I don't believe there's anything supernatural about communicating with the dead," said the Roma King, with his usual relaxed diction and penetrating look. "It's as natural as that china in front of you. We simply don't understand it and haven't developed any proficiency in it, the way we have, say, in making cups and saucers."

"I'm not sure I understand cups and saucers at all," replied Scarlet. "At least how to handle them. I'm forever making chips in the damn things."

Django Pierce-Jones, the Roma King, laughed. "I see. And you never, ever cause harm to the bodies of your patients, do you?"

But his friend wasn't about to take the bait.

"Do you know," he said, abruptly changing the subject, "when it comes to England's contributions to civilization, I don't believe anything equals afternoon tea. As far as I'm concerned, Anna Maria Russell, the seventh Duchess of Bedford, deserves sainthood. And to think that she invented the whole thing not fifty years ago."

Django thought about that for a moment. "I'm always grateful when you teach me things about English culture," he said, "but not, I'm afraid, when it involves avoiding a topic. You are hereby charged and found guilty. Next case!"

The two were, in fact, enjoying afternoon tea at the Langham, one of London's premier hotels. It was Saturday, and the police surgeon was luxuriating in the atmosphere of the hotel with his friend, along with a day away from his surgery and office duties at Scotland Yard.

The business with Macready had taken place four days earlier. It hadn't taken Sgt. Jessey long to find Mrs. Honey's body where Scarlet had told him to look, and he had immediately sent a messenger to the latter's house at One, Beaufort Circle with the news. The coroner for the district, William Higg, had held his inquiry at the Prince of Wales public house on Drury Lane the next day, Wednesday. A finding of willful homicide was easily obtained, Higg had signed a burial form for Mrs. Honey, and Macready had been referred to the summer assizes of the Central Criminal Court.

The Roma King was looking at his friend now with his arms crossed, as though he expected a reply to his last remark. When none was forthcoming, his features assumed that sardonic and gently fatalistic, "Oh-well-that's-that" look that was often on his face, and he took another sip of tea.

Django Pierce-Jones was slightly taller than Scarlet, three years older, and as exotic-looking as Scarlet's complexion proclaimed his Scottish and Anglo-Saxon heritage. Dark and handsome, Django's demeanor and gaze habitually gave the impression of studied interest in what was going on around him, backed by a barely suppressed urge to leap into action. He was blessed with tight black curls that rose high on his head and spilled down luxuriously on either side, covering most of his ears and his collar. He wore his goatee long as well, the moustaches flaring out to each side and curling naturally at the ends. He always dressed in impeccable style and wore tiny wire-rimmed glasses. Anyone meeting him for the first time would be forgiven for taking him for a particularly robust parson, an ambassador from one of the central European countries, or the ringmaster of a circus. He gave the impression of a man of action who nevertheless knew how to preserve his resources.

The two had met three years earlier, when Django had been called in by the Yard to assist in a missing girl case. Django was a natural medium, one who was frequently consulted nowadays during the current wave of interest in spiritualism. This fact, his Romani heritage on his mother's side, and his first name (Scarlet had learned that Django meant "I awake" in Romani), had led his friend to name him affectionally The Roma King. To Scarlet, the hyphenated last name 'Pierce-Jones' seemed the perfect capstone to the man, lending a respectable English gloss to his exotic nature and interests.

The missing girl, incidentally, was never found.

Today's meeting over tea had a purpose beyond the delights of an afternoon at the Langham Hotel. The two men were meeting to discuss the formation of a rather extraordinary club. The idea of this club wasn't theirs to begin with—in fact, they had both been recruited to join two months earlier. It was to be a gentlemen's club, of strictly limited membership and with a particular partiality which was reflected in its name: The Society for Supernatural and Psychic Research. The gentlemen involved—all men of the world—had decided that a medical doctor with a gift for psychometry (they knew through discreet channels about Dr. Scarlet's abilities), and Pierce-Jones, an adept medium who could connect with the spirit world, were prospects too good to pass up.

Django's father was Nicholas Pierce-Jones (changed from the original Neculai Piersic), the chemist and explorer who disappeared in 1872 in the Purus várzea region of the central Amazon basin. Django still lived quite comfortably on the proceeds of his father's best-selling book, *Practical Aspects of Healing from the Plant Pharmacopeia*, published in 1869. The fact that Django was not a man of business or a practicing physician, i.e., that he presumably had more time on his hands than the others, had led the gentlemen to ask if he would serve as Secretary of the Society, and he had accepted.

It was still the age of the great naturalists, many of them amateurs in science, as all the men involved in this project were. In the sciences and natural sciences, the names were well known: Darwin and von Humboldt in biogeography; Banks in botany and van Leeuwenhoek in microscopy; Verreaux in ornithology and Curtis in entomology.

But where were the naturalists in psychic phenomena, and in the occult and supernatural? Aside from Swedenborg (Swedish) and Mesmer (German) who were they . . . and much more important, who were they *among Englishmen*?

The founders of the Society were not concerned with the fashions in magic and mesmerism currently in vogue. They were interested in verifiable psychic phenomena in the world around them. If that uncovered paths that led to the supernatural, well, they would follow those paths. They were amateurs in the best sense, and they possessed the particular zeal of that class—particularly as it revealed itself in privately well-funded clubs and institutions.

The first rule of the club, understood from the start, was that any member could initiate or follow up on a case, including privately employing anyone whose abilities might be helpful. Pierce-Jones would record the Society's activities. At some point the club would publish its findings, though any member was also free to do so on his own if he wished. Dr. Scarlet's particular talent—along with his investigative abilities as a scientist and surgeon—made him a natural choice to be the point man in any investigations. At least, that was the general consensus at this early stage of the proceedings.

Despite his busy schedule, Scarlet was attracted by the convergence of his professional skills, his gift of psychometry, and the Society's interest in the psychic and supernatural. Together, these factors had induced him to sign on at the same time as his friend Pierce-Jones.

These were the admittedly still vague precepts, rules, and understandings in place concerning the new Society at this moment of their meeting at the Langham.

"Here you are," Django said now to his friend, placing a sheet of paper on the table between them. "Our distinguished membership."

Scarlet looked down at the twelve names, along with his own, written on the sheet. The names were, in alphabetical order:

Addams, Adolphus
Blum, Jacob
Borland, John, Sixth Earl of Caversham
Cobb, Charles, Lord Nesbit
Conti, Enzo
Fisher, Holman, Junior
Locke, Thaddeus
Pickering, Julius
Pierce-Jones, Django
Rodney, Sir Hugh
Scarlet, William, M.D.
Scorgie, James
Trippel, Joseph III

"Well, that *is* a distinguished list," said Scarlet, the corners of his mouth turning up slightly.

"Except for the medico, of course. With his trepanning drills and leeches and noxious potions," replied Django.

"Unavoidable in this case, I'm afraid," agreed the guilty party.

Django looked to see if there was any more tea, but there wasn't, and he leaned back comfortably in the tufted chair.

"I've sent the list to all the members. And our calling cards are being printed."

"So, what now?" asked Scarlet.

"We wait for our first case, old fellow," replied Django, looking every bit the rascal.

CHAPTER 3

Dowdeswell's Gallery

By the following week, the wet season had returned to London. When the fog crept in as well, buildings and people became ghosts, and a curious clopping sound heralded odd vertical shapes that emerged slowly from the mist before revealing themselves as broughams, landaus, and hansoms.

Monuments and churches were monsters descending from the clouds which, when no one was looking, attached themselves to the ground. Gas lights did double-duty even in the daytime—not day*light*, for there was none—turning the bridges into magical places that nevertheless seemed to lead nowhere. You smelled the fog and tasted the particles that came with the unhealthy air and you hurried along all the quicker to get where you were going.

But the Season* didn't care! For this was the week Dowdeswell's Gallery opened in its new location, and with an exhibit featuring an exciting young artist. It was true that the geographical distance of the move was slight: a change of address from No. 33, New Bond Street to new premises at No. 160—the previous home of the Le

---

* Editor's Note: The annual period from April – September when the elite of British society came together to meet and be seen. The social whirl included balls, dinner parties, boat races, flower shows, charity events, horse-racing, and test matches. The Season was also the time for the offspring of the nobility and gentry to be introduced into society.

Salon Parisien. Still, for some patrons of fine art in this part of London near Hanover Square, the change was appealing in its return to traditionalism and decorum.

The *British Architect* described the new gallery like this:

> The dark drop, the blood, the comedy, the scent, and the gurgling fountain of Le Salon Parisien are gone, and one of the most beautiful amongst London picture galleries has taken their place. The fine gallery is about 100 feet long, and consists of three compartments, divided off by draped portiéries, and excellently upholstered with drapery, varied between dark blue, green, and sage green and brown.

The Dowdeswell was well known for exhibiting the work of promising young artists of the English school. In the present instance, Messrs. Dowdeswell (father and son) had adorned their new premises with an exhibit of the paintings and drawings of Ambrose Reed, an *en vogue* artist of that school who now joined Whistler, Birket Foster (the illustrator favored by Cadbury's for their chocolate boxes), East, et al., as a featured artist.

In the event, the gallery's grand opening was almost more than the owners—or for that matter, the artist himself—had bargained for. Crowds thronged the place, and the attendants had their hands full shepherding everyone in and out as rapidly yet humanely as possible.

Reed, the artist, found himself answering more questions than he had thought possible, and pressed more closely against members of both sexes in a way that was nearly scandalous. He was shy by nature yet impetuous, and strikingly handsome—he looked remarkably like Chopin—and now he found himself wishing he were somewhere else, or at the least in the company of his fiancée, Elizabeth. But she, unfortunately, was nowhere in sight.

In his mind, a remarkable number of the women present seemed to pay far more attention to him than they did his paintings. Now one of the striking characteristics of Ambrose Reed was that he seemed insufficiently aware of his own remarkable talent. Or did he simply not give any evidence that he gauged it accurately? One couldn't tell. At any rate, for the last hour or so he seemed happy to lend close attention to whomever he was speaking to, without constantly referring to his own work all around him—the common sin of artists everywhere. And it was in the nature of Elizabeth Wilson, his intended, not to care a whit that he did so. But then, she was not present and therefore didn't overhear any of these conversations.

At the moment he was speaking to an elderly couple. The husband (as Ambrose assumed he was) had the stamp of a man who had prospered in one of the trades. The wife was a pleasant, intelligent-looking woman with an open expression who smiled continually and blinked incessantly.

"What's your secret, Mr. Reed?" she asked abruptly now, then blinked quickly twice in succession, as though to indicate a full stop.

Ambrose hadn't a clue how to answer the question. Do artists have secrets? He hadn't the slightest idea.

"I haven't the slightest idea," he said honestly.

The woman looked nonplussed, and the husband dubious.

"Ay, but any one will fetch a right farthing, if the gent thinks it's all-there and he's booked on it. There's a bang up!" the man pronounced enthusiastically.

"Oh, yes!" said a completed baffled Ambrose, with a nervous laugh.

He took the opportunity to look past the man's shoulder toward salvation in the form of Elizabeth. But his savior wasn't present in this gallery. Fortunately, however, the couple moved on while he was looking. He now found himself staring at the nearest painting. It was a gloomy manor house at dusk that he had always thought he'd failed to bring out sufficiently from the background, but he decided that it fit his mood at the moment and that he liked it after all.

He noticed one of the Messrs. Dowdeswell striding purposely

toward the center gallery. To Ambrose, slightly anxious now that he realized he didn't have a secret as all artists should, this movement looked suspiciously like the gallery owner was about to make a short speech. He was sure that such a speech would end with something like, "And now, ladies and gentlemen, I'm sure Mr. Reed would like to say a few words himself."

Mr. Reed would decidedly *not* like to say a few words, or contribute some remarks, or share the sources of his inspiration, or any such thing. For a few seconds he stood rooted to the spot—where could one escape to in an art gallery? He heard the word "gorgeous" spoken in a female voice somewhere behind him, and thought with horror that the woman might be referring not to one of his pictures but to *him*, and the tips of his ears turned red. But escape was still uppermost in his mind. He thought, "I could say I'd gone outside for a breath of fresh air if people say they had been looking for me, couldn't I?" He decided he could, and was trying to remember where the front entrance was when he felt a tap in the small of his back.

"Gangbusters, eh, Mr. Reed?"

It was Walter Dowdeswell, the son.

"Gangbusters!" Dowdeswell repeated, his eyebrows shooting up this time.

His face wore a wide grin as he looked up at the artist; and his eyes had the same eager look Ambrose had noticed upon meeting him the other day, as though he were ravenous to buy up every desirable painting he could find. His hair was again plastered down upon his head, while a long stringy beard emerging from below his chin seemed to creep down visibly in the other direction while Ambrose watched. He stood with one leg bent slightly, as if looking for any excuse to utilize his excess energy and run off somewhere.

Ambrose was getting fatigued just looking at him. He realized, however, that Mr. Dowdeswell was delighted with the size of the crowd on the opening of the gallery's new premises, and was understandably excited.

"You've noticed the red dots on many of the pictures," Dowdeswell proclaimed with confidence.

Ambrose hadn't noticed. But he smiled and nodded. The gallery's commissions, he knew, were sizable.

"I spoke to Lady Blandford, you know," said the little man. "She'd very much like you to come to tea, or something. It doesn't matter. Just arrange a visit, or send her your card or some such thing."

"Couldn't I send her my paints instead? She might have considerable talent of her own!"

Ambrose didn't know why he said such things. They invariably embarrassed him, and he was always a little afraid to say them. But he just blurted them out, sometimes at the most inopportune moments. He didn't understand it at all.

"My dear fellow! You mustn't joke about it. Painting portraits in the right society is quite the thing to do if you want your name to be known. More helpful even than showings like this, I dare say."

Ambrose knew that Dowdeswell was right. Commissioned portraits were not only profitable in themselves; they were magical calling cards in a young artist's career, talismans that always gained entrance. A sitting by the lord or lady in an aristocratic parlour opened doors to other fine houses, more magnificent parlours, and additional distinguished portraits. He thought of the whole thing rather like going down the rabbit-hole in Mr. Carroll's adventures, like Alice growing smaller and smaller as his reputation grew larger.

The idea of it bored him silly. He wanted to paint the *new*—not landscapes in the hundred-year-old English School, all of them crumbling to powder in his mind. He was good at them and his canvases sold well. His *Pastoral Landscape in the Late Afternoon*, for instance, was raved about by the public and a few of the critics (if not the art academies). He was consistently praised for his palette, his vibrant colors, his textures. But more bridges and trees and clouds . . . ugh! He was sick of them and longed to experiment in the styles of France and even America.

Sargent's *Madame X* in particular fascinated him. He had attended the Paris Salon, the official art exhibition of the Académie des Beaux-Arts in 1884 and was fixated by the painting—just as Sargent was said to have been captivated by his model, the American-born Paris socialite Virginie Amélie Avegno Gautreau. Ambrose didn't care about the uproar that had accompanied the painting. People were scandalized by the black dress on a shocking expanse of white skin and the sexually provocative pose of this young coquette. But what did he care about the proprieties! Neither was he awed, as others were, by the French impressionists and their "revolutionary" free use of brush and colors.

But *Madame X*! He was overwhelmed by Sargent's discipline and the assuredness of his hand where the woman's ivory shoulders and arms met the counterbalancing brown background. It was as though the artist had walked boldly at the edge of a precipice, without once falling over!

Let *that* be the type of portrait that leaped from his own brush in those golden mansions. Yet, he knew deep down that such boldness wasn't in him. And of course, the Lady Shallows and Lords Hindbottoms that would commission him would be aghast if he ever showed them anything of the kind.

But Dowdeswell was waiting for an answer.

"It's very kind your speaking to Lady Blandford," Ambrose said. "May I use your name?"

The gallery owner bobbed up on his toes. "Delighted!" he replied, and looked it. Surely, the right connections were as important to dealers as they were to artists. He shook hands heartily with Ambrose, peered at the young artist for a moment as though he himself were a priceless object d'art, then turned without another word and was gone.

Ambrose hardly had time to watch him hurry off, before a voice at his left shoulder said:

"May I be so bold as to interrupt your thoughts, Mr. Reed?"

As it happened, he hadn't had time for any further thoughts, and he sighed with resignation. This was his exhibition, his big day, and he had more or less steeled himself to non-stop conversations about, God help us, his *art*. But the voice was low for a woman, and seemed somehow out of place in his ahead-of-time fantasies about the exhibition. He turned with a small spark of interest to view its owner.

The face seemed as masculine as the voice. The forehead was high, the brows pronounced, with the eyes set deep beneath them. The nose was prominent; and the mouth was wide and firmly set, without the half-smile people usually wore at moments like this. The chin was like the bottom half of a drawn heart, but with the sides straightened, giving it a square and determined look.

Pulling his attention away from the face, he saw a woman of middle age and average stature, with straight shoulders and long arms which hung serenely by her side. Her eyebrows were thin, delicately painted and arched upwards towards the sides of the face—an offset to the robust features that surrounded them. The skin was very white, and the eyes meeting Ambrose's seemed to look at the world with the steadiest gaze he had ever seen. But her hair, in particular, was the most noticeable thing about her at first glance: an enormous cloud of loose black curls that billowed more on each side of her head than at the top. She was small of bosom, the breasts situated somewhat low for a woman of non-buxom proportions. She wore a white dress with billowed sleeves and a black bodice, with a large oval-shaped ruby at the top of the garment where her cleavage would have been. The impression she gave, so incongruous at an afternoon exhibition, was as though she'd just stepped away from a midnight ball.

Ambrose found himself staring rather stupidly, trying to decide whether she was beautiful or slightly hideous and threatening. Why these incongruous concepts would combine in his thoughts wasn't part of those thoughts.

"By all means," he said, smiling slightly, and expecting her to respond in the same way, but without result. He waited, but the woman didn't say anything else, so that he finally ventured: "Are you enjoying the exhibition?"

"You must be very happy," she said, ignoring his question. "Would it be bad form to tell you that I've bought one of your works, I believe it is titled *Lovers in a Wooded Glade*? I don't know the custom when speaking to an artist at his own exhibition, you see."

Was there an accent? If so, it was very slight. Eastern European? The voice was deep, but so quiet that he almost had to strain to hear what she said.

"Well, I'm quite pleased you like it," he replied. "No, not bad form. Any artist likes to hear that his work is appreciated."

"Oh, I appreciate you." It wasn't quite what he'd said.

She was looking at him steadily, her lowered eyelids giving her eyes a languid look, as though she could wait forever for his reply. It was a look that was both indolent and compelling and somehow seemed filled with all the confidence and patience in the world. Of course, he couldn't possibly respond to such a statement.

"And I appreciate your patronage, Mrs. . . . ."

"Bain," she said, filling in the intentional pause. "I am Mrs. Morana Bain."

Bain. Had he heard the name before? He didn't think so. Was there a Mr. Bain or a Lord Bain? That was how people came up to artists at these shows, as a couple. Somehow, however, he doubted that too. The woman seemed too complete a thing in herself, though he wasn't sure what that meant either. From the corner of his eye, he could see people stopping a slight distance away and standing awkwardly, as though wanting to speak to him.

Mrs. Bain noticed as well, and her eyes widened. "But I am keeping you from your public!" she said with a laugh. The change was dramatic and charming and she suddenly seemed younger, though Ambrose hadn't been thinking about her age. "Will you forgive me?"

Ambrose shrugged his shoulders, again at a loss. The question seemed somehow too intimate to come from a complete stranger. Damn these events, he thought. How is one supposed to behave with people coming up to one hour after hour, praising one's work and expecting some sort of reply? He suddenly wanted to escape all over again.

"Shall we make a deal?" she said lightly. "I will release you to your admirers, and you will promise to pay me a visit. We can talk then more comfortably about your work. I live in Lurline Gardens near Battersea Park, on the other side of the river. It's the large brown house at the corner of Forfar Road. Will you come?"

Ambrose said that he would, without any intention of doing so. This woman, he was sure, wouldn't know chiaroscuro from ceiling paint.

"You needn't send your card ahead," she said. "I'm usually at home, or nearby. I can easily be sent word. I will see you then." She walked away in a straight line, not looking at any of the pictures on either side.

That decided him on not going. Who the devil is always at home during the Season? He watched her walking away and suddenly remembered he'd been looking for Elizabeth. Or for the front entrance to go outside for some air, he couldn't recall which.

He found his fiancée with three other people looking at one of his paintings. The two men and the other woman all had their hands on their chins—thinking profoundly about the work, he imagined. He found it comical, and visualized painting this tableau. *Thinking Profoundly,* he'd call it.

"There you are!" said Elizabeth with a warm smile. She took his arm and introduced him to the others. He smiled and forgot their names immediately. He listened to the comments and answered the occasional question, nodding frequently, his face composed into a mask of pleasantry until he was suddenly tired of it all and his jaw began to ache.

"Will you forgive me if I take this talented man away?" Elizabeth said. When she had done so, she said to him: "Have you had enough?"

Ambrose laughed. Of course, Elizabeth had noticed his distress.

"Well, yes," he admitted. "And no. I have to be here, and I'm really enormously grateful to Charles and Walter for the show. Will you stay with me, at least for a while? I feel as though I need a guardian angel."

"What a funny thing to say."

"My dear," he said, placing his hands on her waist and turning her towards him, "you have no idea what it's like being a sheep in the midst of all these wolves!"

Elizabeth's good and lovely face looked back at him, with just a hint of admonishment in her eyes. "No mock humility, please, Mr. Reed! You know this is an adoring public. I'm quite sure you've been in the clutches of attractive women this whole time."

"You'd be surprised, darling," he said. Then he added, "It's been nothing but answering deep questions about the meaning of art the whole time."

Now it was Elizabeth's turn to laugh.

"Come on, Achilles," she said briskly. "Put your armor back on. It's time to leave your tent and go back into battle."

CHAPTER 4

Who Marries a Ghost

Scarlet was drowning in a sea of red.

It rolled in waves in the hall outside; but so far, the operating theatre doors were holding. Some of it had flowed under the doors, however, and he was now ankle-deep in a red tide. The box with sawdust at his feet that was there to catch the blood during surgery was instead floating in blood. His hands were covered in blood; his shirt cuffs were stained with it; and the sleeves of his frock coat were blood-splashed.

The woman on the operating table seemed to have given up all the blood inside her to him and the others doctors. The pink-orange glow of life had long since departed from her, and now she was shrunken and grey. In fact, the whole world seemed to have been drained of its colors. The table and the operating theatre's furnishings were a composition in white, grey, and black. The sheets covering the woman's naked form were white (though they were spotless . . . how could that be?). The woman herself showed extreme pallor. The assisting surgeons' coat sleeves were black. The only color anywhere was the pale blue shade of her lips. And—of course—the sea of red blood that now covered the shoes and pants cuffs of the men standing around the table.

Scarlet noticed that the woman's eyes were still open, and he passed his hand lightly over her lids to close them. Her face was cold to the touch, though the post-mortem temperature plateau meant that she should still be warm this close to death.

Time was clearly playing tricks on him.

He was certain that the woman—her name was Anne Pusey—had been young when she'd been wheeled into the room, not two hours ago. Only nineteen, if he was not mistaken. But the corpse on the table was older than that by a dozen, no, twenty years or more. Could she possibly have aged that much during the operation? Was that the nature of her disease: a mysterious agent that prematurely aged a person when they were opened up? But how could that be? If such an abnormal response existed, surely there would be something about it in the literature.

He thought back to what he'd read in the case book before commencing the surgery. He remembered the notation perfectly: "Patient emaciated and blanched. Chronic inflammation of the rectum and bladder with ulceration of neighboring parts. Fatty liver. Offensive discharge from the rectum." Well, that was all plain enough—never mind how unlikely this would be in a girl of nineteen. She was screaming when they brought her into the theatre, before they administered the chloroform. Then she had begun to gush when the operation began in earnest and they simply couldn't save her.

Now, all of them who had assisted in the surgery were looking down at her. Why wasn't anyone speaking? Why were he and the three other doctors all still standing around the scarred-and-blackened oak operating table, as if the surgery was ongoing? And why were the medical students who filled the spectators' rows still leaning eagerly on the railings, as though something were about to happen, rather than sitting back after the sad anticlimax that had occurred?

Scarlet turned to ask Henry Pollock, the assistant surgeon on his right, if he knew the answer to any of these things. But it wasn't Pollock anymore. It was the dead girl's father. He had never seen the man before, but somehow he knew this was him. His face, noticeable because of its large pores, was ruddy; but the wrinkles at the corners of his eyes and next to his mouth were black, as though encrusted with coal dust. His name was James Pusey, and this was his daughter, Anne, on the table.

"Ye killed her," Pusey said to him in a matter-of-fact voice, as if stating the first part of an equation. And then the second part: "Ye'll have to marry her now." And he added, "She'll tear yer limbs apart if ye don't."

"I can't do that! I'm terrified!" Scarlet heard himself protest.

"Ye doctors are all fools," said Pusey with contempt. "Listen to what I say, man. Ye'r in mortal danger. I'm trying to save yer life. But ye must do exactly as I say."

"Why? Why must I?"

"'*He who marries a ghost is doomed*,'" said Pusey, as if reciting an old moral or maxim.

"But she isn't a ghost!"

"Look!"

Scarlet looked down at the operating table. Anne Pusey's eyes were open. Her father bent down and whispered something in her ear. Her mouth formed the slightest of smiles as she listened. Then she sat up, and swinging her legs around, stepped off the table.

They were side-by-side now, facing her father. Scarlet was aware, now that the dead girl was standing beside him, of how small she was, barely five feet tall. She had tiny feet, auburn-colored pubic hair, and small pointed breasts. But despite her size, the grip of her ice-cold hand in his was strong. He watched her face, but she stared straight ahead with a proud expression on her features, as though she'd always waited for this day: her wedding day. Scarlet was stiff with horror.

"We are gathered here," Pusey began, "to witness the marriage of . . . what's yer first name, son?"

"William . . . William Scarlet." Mad laughter rose in his throat. This was unforgivable—the officiant didn't remember the groom's name! He pushed the laughter back down.

"... to witness the marriage of William and Anne. This union brings together husband and wife fer a joyful commitment to the end of their lives. Or past that, in the case a' one of them. But never mind. May they find together strength and cunning, trust and corroboration, and wedded bliss in their marital burial place. May their bodies be as one ... however they'll manage *that*. We ask a profane blessing of this unsacred rite of the living and the dead, forever and ever.

"Anne, do ye take this man, William, who has killed ye, as yer husband, to have and haunt forever?"

"I do, Father."

"William, do you take Anne, who ye have killed, as yer wife, wedded to her through all the dark nights of yer existence?"

And now for William Scarlet, time ceased the erratic course it had been on through the surgery and its aftermath, and stopped completely. He suddenly understood with complete clarity: *this* was the battle he was to fight from now on. He had made the woman beside him into what she was now. For the rest of his life, he would have to contend with the dead; she was only the first. All of his efforts as a physician and surgeon—the efforts of *all* of them—would never be anything but blood offerings in a vast ocean of death. Today, this ceremony, was the hinge; now he was aware, and he could never look back. This was his fate.

"I do," he said.

His wife Anne turned to him, but didn't kiss him. She smiled for the first time, the blue lips and pallid face framing preternaturally white teeth.

"My enemy," she said.

Scarlet woke up screaming, his eyes searching wildly for blood on his arms and hands. But there was none that he could see.

CHAPTER 5

In Battersea Park

unday morning, the 10th of July, found Ambrose Reed in a location which was unusual for him: south of the Thames. Weekends always featured an art fair in Battersea Park, however, and that was where he found himself this morning.

Most of the exhibitors set up their tents near the Bandstand, which is where he was strolling now, taking his time. Canvases with oils, watercolours, and pencil drawings were prominent, of course. But there were also weavers and conjurers, jugglers and puppet shows, children's games and miniature sailboat races on Ladies Pond. Larger boats were sailing on the Boating Lake, which was connected by serpentine flows of water to the pond.

The day was warm already. To Ambrose, the outdoor setting and the spectacle of amateurs' art was unstudied and refreshing—so unlike the dark and somber confines of the art galleries! To his artist's eye, the colors and costumes exhibited by so many classes of society were as delightful as anything for sale.

He didn't really know why he was here, except that he'd suddenly had an urge to visit the show and stroll in the air of a mid-July morning. Elizabeth was visiting relatives in Hemsby in Norfolk, and he'd successfully declined an invitation to go along. The one hundred and thirty miles each way seemed to him entirely too long a train journey in the middle of the summer.

He found himself strolling past a small tent displaying watercolours of flowers. This was normally something that wouldn't interest him, but one canvas caught his eye. It was of a mass of wildflowers and grasses seen from close-up with, amazingly, royal blue predominating. The artist had opted for a splashy display in an impressionist style, with the flowers at the bottom of the canvas quite indistinguishable except as points of white, orange, blue and green. Ambrose admired the artist's technique very much, but that wasn't what caused his expression to change and his eyes to lose their focus.

The painting brought back to his mind someone that, at one time, he was convinced he would never stop thinking of. But he had stopped; and now she had returned: Mary. His eyes welled with tears; he let out his breath and thought how unexpected his response was.

Mary had loved wildflowers. Three years ago—was it that long already?—he might have bought this painting and taken it home in a cab to his house in Bayswater Road, thinking all the way about how delighted his wife would be. Mary, with her dark curls and non-expressive face that always kept him guessing as to what she was thinking. Small and compact, ever-mysterious Mary Boyle—Mary Reed after they were married—who ruled over him like a distant star, but who nevertheless loved bright sun-dappled wildflowers.

The wife whose death he knew he would never get over, whom he was thinking of unexpectedly now while his fiancée was in the country. How very different Elizabeth was: tall and spare, open of expression, revealing her thoughts to him quietly yet eagerly, while wanting him to share every one of his thoughts. How very good and kind Elizabeth was!

He walked on before the artist who'd painted the watercolours could notice and approach him, because, of course, he had no intention of buying a painting. It would be madness to hang it in his home, a constant reminder of the wife that had been part of his previous, not his upcoming marriage.

After a few moments, he told himself it was just as well. Watching the people in the park was an art show of its own! For many of those around him, it seemed that being seen was an important as anything they saw. He marveled at the varied modes of dress: the bustles and top hats, the accoutrements of colorful shawls on ladies' shoulders, and the shiny waistcoats on the men who considered themselves Cock Robins. Most striking to him was the contrast between the modest black dresses and hats of one class of women, and the other tribe, who wore puffed-sleeved dresses with tightly cinched waists, flowered hats, parasols, and bright boots that constantly drew attention to their owners. Of course, the poorer classes of men and women, with their drab clothes, weren't represented in the Battersea Park Sunday-morning promenade.

He watched a striking woman make her way across his line of sight, conspicuous in a crimson dress with large black horizontal stripes and a matching black choker. She had on a red-and-black hat which—Ambrose was ignorant of the mechanics—somehow gathered all of her abundant black hair underneath the brim. Her serene, confident manner of walking was one that simply invited watching. He had been viewing her in profile; but as she followed the path and began heading in his direction, his eye was caught by a broach containing a large oval ruby pinned to the front of her dress.

"My God, it's Mrs. Bain!" he thought. It was indeed the woman he had met three weeks ago at the Dowdeswell Gallery. He remembered now that she had asked him to visit her at her home, though he had completely forgotten about her request. He had no more than a second or two to look for an escape route before he saw that she'd noticed him.

"Why, Mr. Reed!" she said, in a strong voice and without smiling as she walked up to him. She nevertheless extended her gloved hand towards him.

"You never visited me," she chastised Ambrose. He was momentarily at a loss. He remembered her as being charming—at least at the end of their conversation in the gallery—though she seemed somewhat stern now. He took her outstretched hand and inclined his head in the smallest of bows.

"You've found me out, Mrs. Bain. As you can see, I've been busy scouting out the competition."

"That's a perfectly dreadful lie, and you know it. There's no one here that's remotely at your level. Still, I have found you, as you say, and this time I'm not letting you go so easily."

She slipped her arm through his and they began walking in the same direction she had originally been headed.

"You must tell me what you're working on. I want to hear all about what inspires you and how you consider your own work in light of all the famous French painters everyone is raving about."

"Would any of that interest you?"

"Not in the least. I told you a few weeks ago, didn't I, that it was you I'm interested in, not your paintings?" She gave his arm a slight squeeze. This disoriented him and he felt again, as he had at the gallery, some discomfort at the implied intimacy of the moment. But he dismissed it now, as he had then. This woman, after all, was simply a fan of his work—she'd bought *Lovers in a Wooded Glade*, hadn't she? She certainly seemed to be a foreigner, and so would naturally have a different way of expressing herself.

"I'm afraid I don't know how to respond to that at all, Mrs. Bain. Are you saying you'd like to analyze me, the way the psychiatric doctors are doing these days?"

"I would prefer lunch, wouldn't you?" She then ignored the start of his objection. "The Vendome Park Hotel is cozy, and quite near here. You do realize my home is very close by. Isn't that why you're here in Battersea Park, even if you couldn't work up the courage to pay me a visit?"

It was absurd, of course, and he laughed.

The Vendome Park did in fact take only minutes to walk to, and he soon found himself sitting across a cream tablecloth-covered table from Mrs. Bain in the hotel's dining room. The doors to the terrace were open, letting in a refreshing breeze. It was cool and comforting. No, he thought, I mean comfortable.

He looked across at his luncheon companion now, wondering what looked so different about her. Of course! It was the hair—the distinctive halo of black hair made up of large curls, which had been so abundant and noticeable when he'd first met her. The large soft-brimmed hat she was currently wearing managed to hide it all from view.

He noted again the woman's features, which he'd considered large and masculine when they first met. They didn't seem so much like that now, however, merely . . . what? Strong and assertive, he supposed he'd say. Striking. Perhaps even handsome. Wasn't that what one called a woman with distinctive and attractive facial features? He put her age at thirty-seven or thirty-eight, merely as a guess. There were the mature brows, of course, and the determined-looking mouth and chin.

"You're wondering whether there is a Mr. Bain," she announced, when they'd given the waiter their orders. "I am a widow."

It was a deucedly odd way to start a conversation over lunch!

"Well, you know, I had been wondering that at the gallery. But I decided that since you were alone, and because you hadn't mentioned a Mr. Bain when inviting me to visit, that there wasn't one." There, he thought . . . when it comes to uninvited intimacy, let her take that!

"My husband passed on some years ago. Quite shortly after our marriage, in fact. He was much older than I, and had never been in good health. I only wish I had been able to comfort him more near the end. But his heart simply gave out one morning. He had to post a telegram, you see, and wanted to walk to the office himself for exercise. It was a cold morning and I told him he was being foolish and should send his man instead. But he never listened to me. And of course, I was right."

And that was the end of the old gent, was it? Ambrose thought. He was appalled. It was as though Mr. Bain was a piece of old luggage that had worn out and needed to be discarded. . . . Thank heavens there were art galleries and strolls in Battersea Park on Sunday mornings, and pleasant lunches with young artists to occupy one's time!

"I'm engaged," he more or less blurted out. "Her name is Elizabeth and she's quite wonderful. I'm sorry you didn't have a chance to meet her the other day."

Mrs. Bain gave no outward sign that she'd heard him.

"Isn't this room delightful?" she asked. "I so enjoy lunch on a beautiful day. Then, you can go back outside and enjoy the day some more. Rather like attending a matinée rather than an evening performance, don't you think?"

"Yes, I suppose so," replied Ambrose, frowning.

"And they're ideal for meeting with new acquaintances, of course."

He thought it was time to change the subject.

"Tell me what your interests are," he began. "Aside from pastoral landscapes, that is." The truth was, he was actually interested. He somehow didn't expect her to reply with gossip about social committees, floral societies, charitable institutions, and the like.

"Nothing exciting, I'm afraid. I enjoy furnishing my house in Lurline Gardens, and I keep a country place in Bedfordshire. I like collecting things. Yes, you could call me a collector. It's what widows do."

"I'm afraid I can't accept that, Mrs. Bain. You're still young, and you're quite a handsome woman." Why in the world had he said that last part? Well, it was too late now.

"Morana, please."

"All right, Morana. That's an unusual name."

"Yes. It's Slavic. It's the name of the goddess of winter. It means other things too, but I won't tell you what they are." The corners of her mouth turned up slightly, though it was nothing like a smile. "And now, of course, I must call you Ambrose. May I?"

"I wish you would."

"It's so pleasant to possess a name no one can abbreviate, isn't it? 'Ambrose Reed.' It speaks of intelligence and virility, both."

She certainly had a way of seeming to invite him down the

primrose path, he decided. Leading where, though? He was slightly shocked by the woman's brazenness, and a directness which she somehow made seem like nonchalance. No, not that exactly. Unconventionality, certainly. And a habit of being forthcoming in her speech which was unusual in a widow of her place in society.

On the other hand, there was her name. Morana, goddess of winter. Yes, there was a coldness there which suited her. Perhaps because it was so very different from Elizabeth's warm and selfless personality, he found it oddly attractive.

Their food arrived—a quarter-chicken and cucumbers for Mrs. Bain, stewed beef and potatoes for Ambrose, two glasses of claret. He found he had an appetite. Mrs. Bain ate heartily without any false feminine modesty, smacking her lips frequently. They ate without speaking, and he suddenly had the odd sensation that a thousand years had slipped away and they were two proto-humans feeding hungrily.

They declined dessert, but took coffee. Once they were satiated, the conversation turned to pleasantries that were of no interest to either of them.

"Would you like to take a stroll past my house? So that you can recognize it when you visit," she added, with undisguised mischief. But he declined that too. He had told himself he would get some work done this afternoon.

They parted in front of the beautiful hotel.

"I do look forward to seeing you again, Mr.—Ambrose."

"Goodbye, Mrs.—Morana," he found himself, absurdly, hesitating the same way she had. He watched a boy down the block gathering horse dung from the street with a shovel. Then he turned back to her, nodded and smiled as he shook her hand, and took his leave.

But he didn't get any work done that day, or the next. He simply couldn't get on his game. Well, he knew that it sometimes happened that way. By Wednesday he was painting again.

CHAPTER 6

An Early Chill

lizabeth Wilson returned to London on July the 17th, and Ambrose went to the Wilsons' house in Beatrice Road for tea on Monday, the 18th. It was almost too nice a day to sit inside at tea, even in the late afternoon. The city trotted out its July proudly—it was a month of warm and pleasant weather that changed little day to day. Fog was a phenomenon of the past and future; and though the humidity usually rose in the afternoon during this July, you couldn't see it as you could the fog. It was still London, of course, which meant that rain was always a possibility; but even on those days when it did rain, the sun was likely to return quickly.

Ambrose had been eager to see Elizabeth again. As it happened, there were just the two of them at tea in the drawing room, which both of them were happy about.

"You're looking quite the rosy-cheeked damsel from your stay in the country," he declared as soon as they settled on the settee, the tea things before them on a tray.

He meant it. Elizabeth was fair despite her dark brown hair, and her complexion always benefited from getting outdoors, which he felt she didn't do enough. She had a simple and classic beauty he had always thought—she was one of those women who don't need to do much for it to show. She had remarkably straight eyebrows, light brown eyes, and in his mind, an ideally sized and shaped nose.

Her lips seemed to him exactly the shape that inexperienced artists would recreate in a literal manner: cupid lips that would be too perfect, and that needed an imperfection of some kind to appear real on canvas. At the moment, she had on a black dress with black lace around the edge of a considerable décolletage. Elizabeth had a generous bust which was displayed modestly but unmistakably in dresses like this one.

"You appear to have had some sun too, Ambrose," she told him now. "How is your work progressing?"

Was he imagining it, or was that a subtle criticism that he didn't seem to be getting much work in? Unfortunately, it was true.

"All right. I'm trying some new things." That wasn't true.

"Mr. Dowdeswell, Junior, seems quite pleased with the success of the exhibition. Delighted, in fact."

"Do you mean the successful opening at their new location, or sales from the show?"

"Both, I imagine. Has he made you aware of the pieces which sold?"

"Of course, my dear. Every artist knows that by the close of an exhibition."

Apparently, it sounded like a rebuke to her. "You mustn't be too hard on me, Ambrose. I'm not an artist or gallery owner, after all. Did you do well?"

"Very well. Would you like me to discuss each painting and the sale price?"

Elizabeth frowned. "Why are you speaking to me like this, Ambrose? It isn't like you."

"I'm sorry, darling," he said softly. "I'm probably just tired. From *not* working enough. That's the way it is with artists, you know."

He poured more tea for both of them, eager to get beyond the moment.

She paused, then said in a hearty voice:

"You know, I think Mother is more excited about the wedding than I am! Catherine is being wonderful too, of course. She's the perfect older sister. I'm so lucky to have her." She laughed. "Naturally, Papa talks of nothing but Railway business as usual. I think I'd faint dead away if he asked me anything about the day."

Ambrose looked at her with love. "You will be the most beautiful bride in England this year. I'm the lucky one."

She smiled radiantly, and they both thought that the awkward moment had passed. Ambrose took her hand and kissed it.

"There will never be anyone for me but you," he said.

Elizabeth willed herself to keep smiling. But she thought: Why must he have said that? What about Mary? She was his first wife . . . his first love. There had been *her* for him, hadn't there? And she thought once more of the thing that had always been a source of pain for her: Mary's photograph, which Ambrose still displayed on the mantlepiece in the master bedroom of his home. They had argued about it more than once, but there it remained. Why? She suddenly wanted to cry, but she willed that down too. Then the feeling changed to anger, and she realized she wanted to be alone.

She stood. "Would you mind, darling?" she said. "I promised Catherine we would look at fabrics for her dress."

"Say no more, madam," answered Ambrose, putting his tea cup down and standing as well. He smiled at her. "I believe I may be making my escape just in time."

He was joking. But somehow, he couldn't help feeling that it was true.

CHAPTER 7

Cupid's Revenge

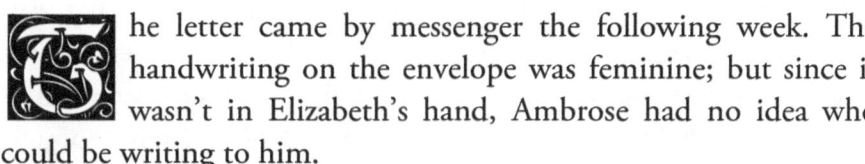he letter came by messenger the following week. The handwriting on the envelope was feminine; but since it wasn't in Elizabeth's hand, Ambrose had no idea who could be writing to him.

The paper inside was the color of sand, and adorned with the image of a black iris at the top. The handwriting was formal and beautiful, with elaborate capitals at the start of each sentence. It was brief, and read:

> My dearest Ambrose. May I request the pleasure of your company at the theatre next Saturday week? A dear friend is appearing and has asked me to attend. The play is Cupid's Revenge. Royal Victoria Theatre. 8.30 pm. Informal private dinner at 14 Lurline Gardens, 6.00 pm.
>
> Yours,
> Morana
> RSVP

Reed was stunned. The invitation itself—to him, an engaged man—was effrontery enough. No, the better word was shameless. And the intimate nature of the salutation and closing! What could the woman be thinking?

Yet, Morana Bain may not have understood how one behaves in London society. But why not? She lived here, and in fact owned a home in a fashionable part of town. Surely, she must understand how she was stepping outside the bounds of decorum. There was no denying at any rate that her act was outlandish and immodest, and of course he wouldn't for a moment consider accepting.

He asked Williams, his butler, to bring him brandy and water, and when it came, sat musing over the brazen nature of some people. At the same time, and precisely because it was something he could never do, he admired the courage on Mrs. Bain's part that made her take a chance like this. Mary, his first wife, was bold in that way, too. She was small but fearless, and insisted on what she thought was her due despite any opposition—a fighter. Like Hermia in *A Midsummer Night's Dream*, he thought. Not entirely, though. Hermia was self-conscious and defensive about her short stature, but to Mary it didn't seem to exist.

These thoughts made him think of the play in the invitation, and he glanced at the note again. *Cupid's Revenge*. He knew it—a typical revenge tragedy of the period by Beaumont and Fletcher. Well, it might be interesting to see whether it was staged in Jacobean or modern style.

By the second or third brandy-and-water, Ambrose was wondering what the evening would be like, and was already past the point of declining the invitation. He wouldn't share a private dinner with Mrs. Bain in her home, though. By God, he drew the line there! Believing that he was still capable of framing a coherent reply, he picked up his pen.

Ten days later, he arrived at the Royal Victoria Theatre a little after eight p.m. He realized immediately that the play must be a hit. Carriages were thick at the entrance, and the lobby crowded. Most of the theatre-goers would already have had dinner—it was the reason for the slightly late curtain times these days. He wished he had done so. The truth was, he thought he'd needed the drinks that he'd had to brace him for the evening more.

Patrons were stealing glances at him in the lobby. He knew well enough that he was handsome and striking in evening dress. But he didn't think that was it. He was sure that his reputation as an up-and-coming artist was the cause of people's notice, especially just a few weeks after the exhibition. He occasionally caught someone's eye, and the two of them, he and the stranger, would exchange a nod. He decided that this would probably turn out to be a pleasant evening; and after all, he was eager to see Mrs. Bain again. The thought had hardly occurred to him since the day of the invitation that he should have told Elizabeth about the meeting, and so he hadn't.

Morana was standing by the doors leading into the house on the far right of the lobby, out of the way of the main body of people but with a view of the street entrance. When he noticed her, she was looking at him, and he realized she had seen him first but didn't want to be the one to come to him.

He smiled and began walking in her direction. Watching her face as he approached, once again he couldn't decide whether she was beautiful or unattractive: her features too large and stern, the face as a whole too unwomanly. It was strange how a man could sometimes struggle to decide between beauty and simply uniqueness regarding a woman's looks.

She wore a burgundy dress, adorned with three bows of the same color, the top one very large but the others becoming smaller as they descended. The neckline was low-cut and straight across, and a mantle of lace fell away like small waterfalls at her bare shoulders. The bodice fitted tightly, and came to a sharp point just below the waist, drawing the eye downwards. The skirts of the dress were fashioned in exactly the opposite way, with a large inverted V-shape that was wide at the bottom but growing narrow as it rose. The middle section was of white fabric the same shade as the shoulder-lace. The effect of the wide-but-narrowing shape—and the white fabric against dark burgundy fabric on either side—drew the eye upwards, to exactly the spot just below the waist that the bodice was pointing down to from above.

Her hands and arms were bare, and she wore a necklace of diamonds and rubies. It was all of a muchness; yet the other ladies present were no less elegantly attired.

He reached her and, without thinking, kissed her outstretched hand.

"You look quite lovely," he said, again unthinkingly.

"Not too obviously a widow?"

He had no idea what she meant, and chose safety.

"I'm looking forward to the play. Thank you for the invitation. Do you know it?"

"I'm afraid I don't," she said, slipping her arm in his as they turned toward the entrance to the house. "I'm counting on my companion to explain anything I don't understand."

There was hardly the need for that, it turned out. The plot of *Cupid's Revenge* was straightforward and simple. Unlike many of the Jacobean dramas, there weren't so many subplots that one became easily lost.

Leontius, the Duke of Lycia, decides to grant his daughter Hidaspes any wish she desires on her birthday. She demands that her father issue an edict outlawing the cult of Cupid that is dominant in the kingdom, and granting her wish, the Duke decrees that the god's temples be destroyed and his statues pulled down. Cupid, as jealous as any of the gods, vows revenge. Since he *is* Cupid, that revenge takes the form of desire—some consummated, some unrequited. Bacha, an attractive widow, takes the Duke's son Leucippus as her lover; but when he throws her over, she sets her sights on his father, and the power and riches she will gain as Duchess in the kingdom. The Duke in turn is infused with lust for Bacha. Eventually, he dies naturally. The villainous Bacha stabs her former lover Leucippus the son to death, then herself.

"I should hardly think there was enough stage blood to cover the stage when plays like this were originally performed," Morana said when the curtain fell.

"You're probably right," Ambrose replied. It was the first evidence of any humor in Mrs. Bain and he was delighted. They walked silently, arm in arm down the ornate stairway from the dress circle to street level.

"I would like to enjoy some air before we go home," she said. "The groom will wait for us." The night was warm and pleasant as they stood to the left of the theatre's main entrance, watching people getting into the carriages that rolled up one by one.

"Do you believe the gods have such power?" Morana asked him suddenly.

Ambrose laughed.

"I hadn't thought about it. They haven't, though, not for the last two thousand years at least."

"You're joking. But I meant it as a serious question."

"You mean concerning free will and all that?"

"What I mean is fate. In the play, the son and the father were *fated*"—she emphasized the word—"to act the way they did, don't you think?"

"Well, no, rather. It was simply revenge, wasn't it?"

"No, it wasn't. It was their actions that caused the god—Cupid—to do what he did."

"Then, Cupid too was fated to act the way he did."

"You are clever," she told him. "I think the . . . do you say 'playwrights,' revealed more than they thought they were showing through that plot, however. About how we are playthings of forces larger than ourselves." Then she shrugged. "But never mind. We view murkily through the glass."

"We see through a glass, darkly," he corrected her.

"And the woman," she said, obviously wanting to dissect the play some more. "Bacha. What do you think of her?"

"A wonderful performance. The danger, of course, is to portray a Jacobean villain with too broad a stroke. All one color, you might say."

"I don't mean the actress," Mrs. Bain corrected him. "I mean the character."

"Oh, she was clearly evil."

"And what is evil?"

That gave Ambrose pause. "Well, I suppose you'd say, serving the purposes of evil."

"You don't think she was simply satisfying her lust? For the prince and riches, both?"

"Well, that of course," agreed Ambrose, starting to feel somewhat out of his depth.

"What do you think of that lust? For the younger man?" Again, there was almost a smile on her lips.

Now it was his turn to shrug. "Perfectly natural," he replied. "Why not?"

"You surprise me, Ambrose." After a pause, she asked: "Do you think he had a choice? 'Free will,' as you mentioned a moment ago."

"Yes, I do. There is always a choice in such things."

"Yet she was so attractive—the character, I mean."

"Indeed."

"And clever."

Ambrose laughed. "Then I suppose he didn't have much of a choice, did he? The spider and the fly!"

"Or fate," said Morana. "Or one might say, forces much more powerful than his human will. So, I suppose we are right back where we started."

"You're a philosopher."

"I am a lady who is rather cold," she said, though to Ambrose the evening was still warm. He raised his arm and the groom immediately came up in Mrs. Bain's brougham.

Since they were already south of the river, it made sense to drop her first at Lurline Gardens before the coach took him home to Bayswater Road. When they arrived at her house, she thanked him for the evening, then leaned in and brushed his cheek with her lips, filling his head with her perfume.

It was only when the carriage rolled up to his front door and he was reaching for the handle that he remembered Morana's invitation to attend the play with her. He'd forgotten to ask during the performance who her friend was in the cast of *Cupid's Revenge*. And of course, they hadn't sent word via the stage door to meet anyone afterwards.

It didn't matter, he decided. He caught the scent of her perfume in the cab's interior, and realized he wanted to see her again.

CHAPTER 8

Butter and Cream

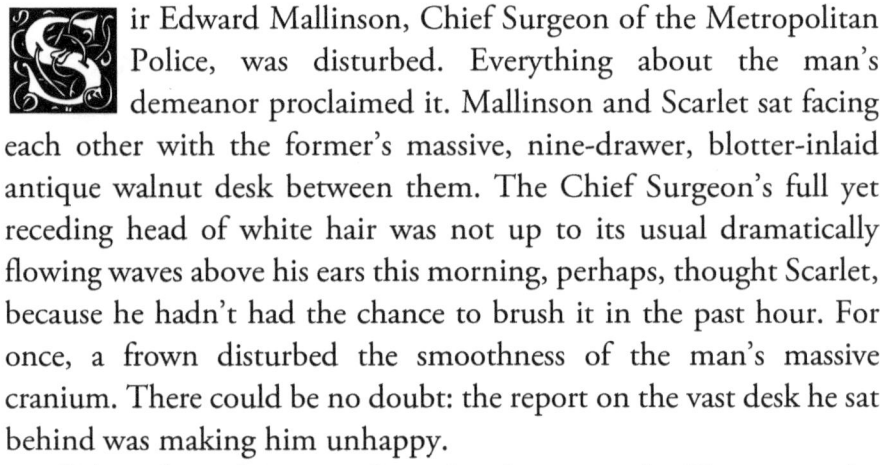ir Edward Mallinson, Chief Surgeon of the Metropolitan Police, was disturbed. Everything about the man's demeanor proclaimed it. Mallinson and Scarlet sat facing each other with the former's massive, nine-drawer, blotter-inlaid antique walnut desk between them. The Chief Surgeon's full yet receding head of white hair was not up to its usual dramatically flowing waves above his ears this morning, perhaps, thought Scarlet, because he hadn't had the chance to brush it in the past hour. For once, a frown disturbed the smoothness of the man's massive cranium. There could be no doubt: the report on the vast desk he sat behind was making him unhappy.

"I have here the report from Sgt. Jessey on the Honey murder case," he intoned in the calm voice that somehow to Scarlet always conveyed the impression of butter and cream. Nothing, however disturbing, would ever alter *that*. Only someone who knew him well would realize the extent of his current state of disapproval.

"Apparently, you assisted the sergeant in gathering evidence of the suspect's; let us see, what is his name—yes, Timothy Macready's, crime."

Mallinson was the only person Scarlet had ever encountered who spoke in commas and semicolons. It was simply part of his meticulous speech, like creating a precise red line with a scalpel. And now it was time for the first cut.

"Would you like to explain what your assistance entailed?"

Scarlet seriously doubted whether his superior wanted to hear him say: "Oh, it involved reading the man's mind, sir." He was still considering an alternative when Mallinson spoke again.

"You are an assistant chief surgeon with the Yard, are you not?"

This was so much like a parent saying, "Did I not tell you to leave the biscuits alone?" that he had to compose himself before answering.

"I am."

"And would you share with me the duties incumbent upon that position, as you understand them?"

Rather than continuing with this charade, Scarlet asked a question of his own.

"Is there something in Sergeant Jessey's report you would like to discuss, sir?"

"Indeed," Mallinson replied at once, "there is. It has to do with the apparent belief you have, Mr. Scarlet, that you are a *fortune teller*. In fact, I'm amazed that you didn't foretell beforehand what I wanted to discuss with you this morning." His face suddenly lit up. "Wait a moment! Perhaps we needn't discuss this after all. You can simply read my thoughts and then leave. Shall we give it a try?"

It was the old Ring a Ring o' Roses game, thought Scarlet. Goodness knows it was something the two of them played often enough. *Round and round we go! . . . We all fall down!*

"This had nothing to do with the sergeant," Scarlet said now. "It was my idea entirely to interrogate the suspect."

"Kindly don't bother lying to me," said Mallinson. "I've had the whole story from Jessey. I know he summoned you to the place where he was holding this McGregor."

"Macready, sir."

"And you miraculously discerned—from a mere touch, I understand—that a murder had been committed by this man. *Miraculum satis.* But you also knew where the body was hidden. I am simply in awe of you, Mr. Scarlet!"

"Is there a problem with the evidence?" asked the other, knowing the answer.

"You know damn well, there isn't. The problem is in your methods, sir. You are a doctor and a surgeon. Your duties in this organization involve your medical skills, knowledge, and experience. They do not call upon you to conduct investigations into the occult and the supernatural!"

This was going too far. Mallinson's criticisms of his actions on the job were valid. But they must stop there.

"If you're referring to the Society I belong to, sir . . . "

"Confound your damn Occult Society, or whatever it's called That is no concern of mine. What *is* my concern is what you do while carrying out your duties at the Yard. My God, man—your job isn't investigating crime at all. You know bloody well it isn't!" He was really heating up, thought Scarlet, to use language like this. "If you want to quit and apply to the detective division, we can discuss it. But I won't stand for my top assistant surgeon running around telling fortunes."

He held up his hand as Scarlet tried to respond.

"And I don't care to hear about your peculiar abilities. Keep 'em to yourself, and don't allow them to intrude on your official duties. This isn't the first time we've discussed this, as you well know. Do we understand each other, Mr. Scarlet?"

"I believe we do, sir," said Scarlet, and stood. "Is there anything else?"

"I know you don't like me," said Mallinson, gathering up the report in front of him. "The truth is, I don't care. And you shouldn't either. You have a job to do, and so do I. I expect you to carry it out in the traditions of the medical office of the Yard. Your duty and mine is to serve that office to the best of our abilities, regardless of any personal sacrifice that may entail. Good day, sir."

The truth was, thought Scarlet as he stood up to leave, he couldn't argue with any of that.

CHAPTER 9

The Society Sallies Forth

id-August had arrived with momentous news: the initial meeting of The Society for Supernatural and Psychic Research would talk place on the first Friday in September. Now the day had arrived, and Django Pierce-Jones (as designated Secretary) found himself wondering what remarks and decisions might result from this evening's gathering. He thought it rather a delicious irony that though he was a medium, he had no idea.

It had been two months since he and Scarlet had met for tea and Django had handed his friend the final list of the new Society's membership. The eleven other names on that list were busy men of business, however, and coming up with a date for their first meeting had been harder than he had anticipated.

All was now well, however. The senior statesman of the Society, Lord Nesbit, had contributed an upper room in his house in Russell Square where they could meet. For this first meeting, Lord Nesbit would be hosting dinner downstairs in his home, after which they would all retire upstairs for Society business.

The main item in tonight's agenda—which had without doubt created excitement in the breast of each member—was choosing the Society's first case! For that reason alone, thought Django, this should be a night to remember.

Everyone was on time for Lord Nesbit's dinner, and the cuisine and atmosphere were both remarkable. Everyone expected that the man's hospitality and fare would be exceptional, and that had proven to be the case. Of course, a few of the Society's members had dined there previously, but most had not.

During the courses of soup, fishes, main entrées, puddings, cheeses, fruits, and assorted wines, liqueurs, and coffee, Django had watched the men assembled around him with a sense of wonder. It was, he thought, a group of gentlemen worth knowing in any context. Each was successful, and each seemed a master of his fate. At any minute now, he thought, one of them would give a signal, and they would all leap up and call for their horses and armour, sallying forth to engage their enemies whether natural or supernatural!

When the group, with much greater modesty than that in the event itself, ascended the main staircase after dinner, he found himself as Secretary hoping that every man's voice would be heard. Well, they'd soon find out.

The upstairs room they retired to seemed ideal for their meeting. For a second parlour, it was extremely large and ornate, making Django wonder what the front parlour must be like. The room was long and rectangular, with stained-glass windows at the street end. It was built of some heavy dark wood, and featured a ceiling of hammered tin. A long boardroom table occupied the center of the room, and underneath it lay a vast oriental rug in an intricate design of red, maroon, purple, and white wool. The entire space was almost aggressively masculine. Everything carried weight, including the armchairs, which were obviously men's chairs with high backs and arms. A round gold-painted ceiling fixture with brown beadwork around the edges was centered high over the table, and a crystal chandelier with cleverly hidden gas jets hung down from its center. Though it was early September, a robust blaze filled the fireplace behind a façade of polished black marble, underneath a heavy mahogany mantlepiece featuring carvings of lions' heads at either end.

The members seated themselves at the table in no particular order. Decanters of madeira, sherry, whisky, brandy, and water were already in place. Cigars made in Seville from Cuban leaf awaited everyone, resting in cigar boxes of birch trimmed with ivory. Most of the men immediately poured themselves a drink or lit up.

Django remained standing and called the meeting to order. Then he took his seat, with a new journal, a stub pen—which he was skilled at using—and blue-black ink at his side, ready to transcribe whatever debate would follow.

Not surprisingly, John Borland, Earl of Caversham and the only MP in the Society, was the first to speak. Django thought that he looked and sounded the part so entirely that he might have stepped down from a painting in the halls of Westminster to attend the meeting.

"May I remind the honourable members of my previous remarks?" he began. "I said then that we should be a research society that studies and records historical events, not a band of rovers running around the country sniffing for evidence of the supernatural. We should probably publish a book or two detailing our findings. Does everyone agree?"

Julius Pickering, founder of the Pickering line of grocers, responded. He was a short, stout man in a middle-class brown suit with an abnormally large black bow-tie adorning the top of it.

"Don't be ridiculous, John," he began. "This isn't Parliament. I doubt there's anyone honourable here." [Laughter] "We're not a bunch of *librarians*, for goodness's sake," he protested, making a face. "Anyway, I thought this was already decided upon. We're to undertake investigations into occult phenomena of all types. Isn't that our mutual interest?"

"Hear, hear!" This was Holman Fisher, Junior—a tall thin young man whose moustache was small but whose enthusiasm wasn't. In fact, he repeated himself: "Hear! Hear!"

"I believe," Scarlet interceded, "that our agreement concerning tonight, was that each of us would nominate a recent phenomenon that the Society would consider investigating. Was that your understanding, Mr. Secretary?"

Django nodded judiciously, but said nothing.

"Yes, I have something!" said Fisher, pointing his index finger in the air. "I don't recall where I heard about it. Anyway, a man woke up suddenly one night, thinking of his uncle. The next day, he found out that his uncle had been killed in a train wreck *at exactly the moment he woke up!*"

"Didn't Dickens write about that?" asked Lord Nesbit.

"You're thinking of his short story about a conductor who foresaw his own death," responded Thaddeus "Teddy" Locke, a tight-faced banker who was very good at quashing people's ideas.

"No, no, it was a signal-man!" said Joseph Trippel III, an eager young fellow with beautifully coiffed hair and, tonight, the stiffest of high collars. "In fact, I think that's the title of the story."

"Well, it's rot, anyway!" contributed Pickering. "That idea is as common as dirt. Everybody has a story about someone with a premonition of someone else dying, always at the exact moment the person wakes up or feels a pang in their bum or some such thing. It's rubbish!" he finished with a dismissive wave of his hand.

"I think," Django stepped in, "that we should approach this in an orderly fashion. Let each gentleman speak in turn and make their nomination. Then, we can vote on which case we'd be most interested in exploring. Is that acceptable?"

It was. Not a single man present thought that all the members of the Society had come with a nomination ready, as they were supposed to. Still, there should enough incidents for them to at least get started and, with luck, decide upon their first case.

Enzo Conti, the Italian vintner and exporter sporting a high-buttoned blazer, a magnificent still-black caterpillar of a moustache, and a combed-over hairstyle, was the first to contribute.

"I hear the story of people in a village, they all suffered from the black spiders," he said. "The spiders ate up the livestock, then came for the villagers. They built a post and trapped the king spider in it, and closed the hole with mud or something."

"I'm afraid that's another short story," said the man who was perhaps the most famous architect in England, Sir Hugh Rodney. He had thinning grey hair which seemed to have been precisely parted with a knife or something equally sharp, an equally neatly-trimmed beard, and a steady look of intelligence and business. "It takes place in Switzerland. Quite interesting actually, but it doesn't suit our purposes."

"I heard something," offered Jacob Blum, the shipbuilding magnate, his heavy-lidded eyes looking as always like he was half-asleep. "A young couple bought a house in the Cotswolds. Now, every night a young mother walks through their bedroom with the head of a child in her hands."

"What!" exclaimed James Scorgie, the red-headed and red-bearded owner of *The Daily Post* newspaper. "What mother carries the head of a child? It's always her own head."

"It could be her child's head," protested Trippel. "If she had murdered it."

"Well, the county records would show it, wouldn't they?" suggested Lord Nesbit. We'd only have to look them up and see if the child was buried without a head."

"Don't be ridiculous, Charles," admonished Sir Hugh, waving his cigar in the air. "It's another wives' tale." He turned to Blum, the shipbuilder. "Do you know who this young couple is, Jacob? Do you have any specifics at all?"

"'Fraid not."

There was a gap in the conversation. Everyone present, it seemed, was beginning to realize that their task would not be as easy as they had anticipated.

"Is there nothing else?" asked Django, not bothering to keep the disappointment out of his voice. Unfortunately, his question produced nothing but chagrined looks around the table. A few of the men developed a sudden thirst, or discovered that the makings of a cigar were particularly interesting, once you took a close look at one.

"Well," said Fisher, the enthusiastic young man, breaking the silence at last. As a dozen questioning looks were directed his way, he offered: "There *is* a true story I heard about."

"Marvelous!" said Scorgie, the note of sarcasm in his voice obvious. "A *true* story at last!"

"My cousin told it to me," said Fisher. "She heard it from her friend's fiancé, who knew the farm where the fellow in the story worked." Scorgie snorted audibly, which Fisher ignored. "A farrier had a dream, you see, for three nights running. A voice, or an owl—I'm not clear which it was—told him to make a journey to London and stand on a certain spot on Southwark Bridge for three nights running. On the third night, one of the Queen's councilors would approach him on that spot and convey important information to him." With that, Fisher raised his eyebrows and sat back in his chair.

"Yes?" said Scarlet.

"That's it?" asked Pickering.

Adolphus "Dolly" Addams, an aristocratic horse breeder who hadn't spoken until now, said soothingly, "It was only a dream, though, wasn't it, old fellow?"

"No, it wasn't!"

"Well, how d'you know that?"

"He did it. The farrier, I mean. He went to London for three nights and stood on Southwark Bridge."

"And what happened?" asked Trippel.

Fisher's eyebrows shot up even higher. "On the third night—in exactly that spot on the bridge—a police constable came up to him. 'Be on your way, lad,' he told him, 'or you'll regret it, as you'll wind up in a cell.' The farrier said he realized then that his life was changed, just as the dream foretold."

One by one, he looked back at the twelve pairs of eyes that were staring at him incredulously.

"Bloody hell!" said Pickering with disgust. Thankfully, however, no one laughed.

It was at that moment that Lord Nesbit's butler, John Dixon, who had entered the room a few minutes earlier to refresh the liquors and water, leaned down to his employer and said something to him in a low voice. Lord Nesbit was known as something of an eccentric, and the freedom he granted his servants was considered scandalous. His face brightened now, however, and he said: "By all means, Dixon. Go ahead."

Standing straight as a ramrod, the butler addressed the Society.

"Beg pardon, gentlemen. My employer has given me permission to speak. Understanding, as well as I could, the needs of the Society as it prepared for its first meeting, I have been keeping my ears open. Indeed, I have—if you gentlemen will forgive me—initiated a few inquiries among the household staff. If you will allow me, I will tell you a story I have heard, which I am told is quite true."

Encountering no resistance, Dixon told the following remarkable story.

A Mr. and Mrs. Alistair Newcombe (of Bucks or Hertfordshire, Dixon thought), were currently being plagued by the ghost of their seventeen-year-old son James, who recently died of typhus. The couple were heartbroken at the boy's death, as he was their only child and their hope for grandchildren. A few months after their son's passing, which is to say recently, his ghost began appearing in their bedroom. It happens on most but not all nights, and always in the same way:

Mrs. Newcombe awakens from sleep, and there is her son's ghost, standing at the foot of the bed. He doesn't say anything, just looks at his mother sadly, but she says she knows what he wants. She says she can hear him speaking inside her head.

"Oh, Mother . . . Mother! Put me back in me own bed."

The first time it happened, half-asleep and forgetting that their son was dead, she said to her husband: "Alistair, Jax (for James) is out of bed. Go put him in't."

The next morning, she awoke with the terrible feeling that her son had been taken out of his grave. She would not sit for breakfast nor do anything else until they had gone to the churchyard. They hadn't yet put up any stone on the grave, but of course they knew exactly where it was. When they arrived at the burying place, they saw a tombstone with another name on it standing at the head of the gravesite!

"That's the true story," finished Dixon. "It seemed to me, if I may say so, gentlemen, a suitable case for the Society's investigation."

The men around the table and in armchairs absorbed Dixon's 'true story' for a few minutes. For it seemed at least worthy of the group's consideration.

"Well, gentlemen?" Blum, the shipping magnate, said at last. By which everyone understood him to mean: "Shall we take this on?"

"I think not," said Teddy Locke, the banker. "This is a simple business transaction for monetary gain."

The group sat up at that—for they all knew that if anyone would recognize 'a business transaction for monetary gain,' it would be Teddy. He then explained.

"It's not an uncommon ploy. The gravedigger sells the same plot someone has recently been buried in to another buyer, without informing the church or county treasurer. A reopened grave that had been recently dug will hardly be noticed, you see, when he plants a second body in it. All goes well until one or other of the parties decides to put up a headstone. Then, questions start being asked. Typically, the gravedigger then digs up one of the corpses some dark night, most likely the one not about to get a headstone, and re-buries it someplace else. Obviously, the fellow's timing was off in this instance. I'd be surprised if the gravel-scratcher involved hasn't already been arrested and restitution of some kind ordered by the assizes."

The members of the Society looked at each other, of one mind at last.

Apparently, they wouldn't be sallying forth just yet.

CHAPTER 10

The Disappearing Children

The first one was in June, at the time of the Queen's Jubilee. On the early evening of the 21st—the summer solstice—a nine-year-old street urchin named Walter Morrissey went missing in the Potteries and the Piggeries district of Notting Hill. Given that neighborhood (whose old name was Cut-Throat Lane), and the boy's situation in life, his disappearance produced hardly a ripple of concern or even awareness.

Jacob's Island, the slum in Bermondsey, nearly eight miles to the east and on the other side of the Thames, was the scene of the second disappearance on the 20th of July. This one was clearly an abduction, as twelve-year-old Sarah Gates was seen walking with a suspicious figure and was immediately missed by her family. It was late dusk on a moonless night, however, and the description the police received was nothing more than "a person dressed in black." The investigators in M Division could do nothing with it.

In mid-August, two eleven-year-old boys, Isaiah Trawley and Richard Gibb, constant companions described as "vagrants" and occasional dung-sweepers, vanished into thin air on another dark night in Southwark, less than two miles from Bermondsey on the South Bank of the Thames. They were last seen leaving the notorious St. Saviour's Union Workhouse, from which they frequently escaped. This time, however, they never returned.

The next night, Mary Bird, age two, disappeared from her crib in Maida Hill, seven miles away in north-central London. This time the neighborhood was an affluent one, with servants who lived in the home. Yet Mary's abduction was so silent that she wasn't missed until the following morning.

On the evening of the 17th of September, two more children, Magdalena Murphy and Henri Aubert, disappeared from the face of the earth. They had lived and played, respectively, in the adjacent areas of Islington and Dalston, six and seven miles farther north from Maida Hill, and in East London.

The time intervals between the children's disappearances, the far-flung locations throughout the metropolis in which they took place, and the different jurisdictional divisions in which the vanishings occurred, initially kept them from being considered as linked by the Yard. By September, however, the Metropolitan Police suspected that they had a string of child abductions, and most likely murders, on their hands.

The officers and detectives' progress in investigating the disappearances was frustratingly slow. They reasoned that the perpetrator—seen only once at dusk and from a distance—was probably a person of standing and genteel appearance. Such an individual could move with ease in the slums, though the opposite would not be the case in an affluent neighborhood. It would be unreasonable to assume, for instance, that someone of poor dress and habits could frequent the wealthy neighborhood of Maida Hill, where little Mary Bird was abducted, without being noticed—and indeed, get close enough to the Birds' home without arousing suspicion. Given the diverse areas of the city in which the abductor worked, they also felt it was not a local stalker hunting in a familiar habitat among prey he or she knew well. For the same reason, the suspect would need some form of ready transportation—whether that meant the underground, the Metropolitan Rail system, or cabs. This was an unlucky turn, as it immediately ruled out all the local nonces who were known to molest children in their neighborhoods.

Women occupied the detectives and inspectors' minds as much as men. They reasoned that a woman, especially a well-dressed and -spoken lady, would have been able to gain a child's trust far more easily than a man.

Police constables in each of the affected districts began to knock on doors and to quietly pull aside anyone who came to their attention. Known offenders found themselves paying unintended visits to station houses, and having uncomfortable conversations inside them. The Yard's meagre funds were called upon to reward the blowers or Welshers who, though criminals themselves, made a secret part-time income as police informers.

Word had spread quickly throughout the Metropolitan Police, and Scarlet, among others, knew the force was facing the blackest of scenarios: a repeat killer of young children, clever enough to strike silently without warning, and resourceful enough to dispose of the bodies so that not a single child had been found. He was of two minds about the progress of the investigation. Finding the children alive would be a Godsend, even if it meant they were being held for evil intent, for their lives would be spared. On the other hand, as a surgeon he knew that one or more of the bodies might give up clues to the killer during the post-mortem examination. In either case, he could only imagine the agony that the families of the children were going through.

As of this moment, they had a single weak clue: a shadowy figure seen leading one of the children. A dark shape in the London dusk, neither male or female, wearing a coat or cape that could belong to either sex. The witness might just as well have said "non-human," for the results at this stage would have been the same.

It was a somber time for the Yard, even as a Queen Victoria Police Jubilee Medal was planned for officers who had been on duty during the celebrations three months earlier. Sir Charles Warren, Commissioner of the Metropolitan Police since the previous year, had never been above enlisting unorthodox resources when necessary; and given the headlines being written about the missing children, he wasn't about to suddenly become timid and hidebound to regulations. And so, Scarlet's fellow Society Member, Django Pierce-Jones, was brought into the case.

Those members of the force that frowned upon a psychic's help in an investigation kept their thoughts to themselves now. At any rate, Django was a popular figure in the Yard. He always kept a quiet profile until he was called upon; though he would be the first to admit that he didn't believe in hiding his light under a bushel. He used his considerable skills—especially in séances, his specialty—to bring forth anything that might help investigators in their enquiries. Yet he invariably gave the police full credit afterwards. He was shrewd enough to know that a medium who allowed the authorities to claim success would be valued—and sought after—by those same men.

As it happened, he made one contribution to the case now which Scarlet considered invaluable.

The two were standing over Scarlet's working space in his small office at the Yard. A better word than 'office' would have been 'closet'—one with a battered desk that took up so much room Scarlet had to walk all the way around it to get to his chair.

Django had just torn a sheet from Scarlet's journal and now he slapped it down on the desk. "Here, look at the dates," he said, then wrote the following:

21st June
20th July
18th August
19th August
17th September

"Anything strike you?" he asked. Scarlet saw it at once.
"Roughly monthly intervals."
"Yes," said Django. "Specifically, the lunar cycle. "Once I recognized it, I looked up these dates. There was a new moon on

each of them—and most of the disappearances were on the first night of that new moon. The Trawley and Gibb boys, and the Bird girl, were on consecutive nights, which were the only two nights of that moon in August." He looked up. "We're dealing with someone for whom the new moon is important."

Scarlet thought about that.

"Just because of the darkness? Or as part of a ritual?" he asked.

"I don't know," replied Django, then frowned. "But it doesn't make sense. In astrology, the new moon is a time for renewal, for reflection, for setting intentions for the next cycle . . . that kind of thing. It's the full moon that is associated with the time of highest energy, and for allowing for openness and receptivity. And, of course, for manifestation."

"Like werewolves?"

"Well, yes. But there are no indications of anything like that here. That would involve more frenzied energy, and we'd certainly see evidence of it." Django paused, then added: "There's another thing that worries me, though."

"About the new moon?" asked Scarlet.

"Yes," replied the Roma King. "It's also a time for planting seeds for the future."

CHAPTER 11

Elizabeth and Catherine

"I'm so very unhappy," said Elizabeth Wilson.

"Oh, my darling," her sister Catherine replied with feeling. "I know you are."

The two women were holding hands—as like and unlike each other as sisters often are. They were seated on the settee in the Wilsons' drawing room, which at this time of the morning was especially bright and cheerful, with its mint-green walls and blue chairs and rug. Elizabeth, her pale skin set against a tea gown of black with a red floral design, was a dark accent amid the morning light filtering through the broad windows. Her sister Catherine, two years her senior, was dressed in opposite fashion, in a white dress which made her rose complexion and naturally wavy auburn hair all the more striking. Elizabeth thought (as she often did) how very beautiful Catherine was, and she almost smiled amid her misery.

"I'm quite sure that he loves you," said Catherine, giving her sister's hand a small squeeze.

"So *was* I," replied Elizabeth simply.

For a brief instant, Catherine thought of mentioning that, after all, Ambrose hadn't called off the engagement. But she realized immediately that that would be a remarkably stupid thing to say.

"And you believe it's this older woman, this Mrs. Bain, that is distracting him?"

"I don't 'believe' it, Cathy—I've *seen* them together! At the

Dulwich Picture Gallery. I'd heard rumors, but to see them, arm in arm! I was mortified, of course."

"Oh, my dear."

"What was I to do? I could hardly walk up to them and introduce myself to her: 'Ambrose, darling! How nice to see you here. And who's this mature and dark-looking woman hanging onto you?'"

"Stop, Liz. Sarcasm doesn't become you. It's perfectly awful, of course."

Catherine saw no reason to dress up the sordid truth, that Ambrose apparently *was* stepping out on her sister. It was a perfect scandal, of course.

"Do you think it's because he's suddenly become so popular?" she asked Elizabeth now. "And this woman is simply a potential patron that Ambrose is courting? . . . Oh, I'm sorry, Liz. What an awful word to use!" She kept to herself the fact that Ambrose was also strikingly handsome as well as popular.

"What am I going to do?" asked Elizabeth plaintively.

"What is there *to* do? You must confront him about it, of course."

Elizabeth let go of her sister's hand and wrung her own two hands together.

"I'm not brave like you are," she told Catherine. "And . . ." she hesitated.

"Confrontational?"

"No, not at all," Elizabeth protested. "I suppose I would have said direct."

"And outspoken and entirely too equal-minded where men are concerned for any gentleman to have proposed marriage?"

Elizabeth smiled. She pictured Catherine weeping in the evenings at her lack of a husband, and this time laughed outright. "You know what I mean," she said.

"I do, and it's one of your best qualities, dear sister," said Catherine. "You're demure and loyal and sweet, in addition to your beauty. And you know I'm eternally jealous of you. However, in this situation . . ."

"I must confront Ambrose about this other woman," Elizabeth volunteered the information herself. "What else can I do? I can't let things go on as they are now."

Catherine didn't say anything for a moment, allowing her sister the time to convince herself of what she was saying. It seemed to work.

"I must, mustn't I?" asked Elizabeth.

"Yes, you must. And if it's all just a misunderstanding, you must allow your fiancé the benefit of the doubt, and the chance to tell you so."

Elizabeth thought about that for a few seconds.

"But you don't believe that, do you?" she asked Catherine.

"No. I'm afraid I don't, my darling," came the honest reply.

CHAPTER 12

Three Scenes in Finsbury Park

[Scene 1: Finsbury Park, in north-central London. Elizabeth and Ambrose are discovered sitting on a bench. There is a pedestrian path directly in front of the bench, and a broad lush lawn behind it which is brilliantly green.]

lizabeth Wilson was watching a fast-moving cloud mass about to envelope the sun. She thought dully that her life was on display up there in the sky, with her own happiness winking out. She was merely an observer.

She and Ambrose had walked from the Wilsons' home, Nine Columns, on Beatrice Road in the Finsbury Park neighborhood of London to the park itself. Now they were sitting on a bench on the lawn near the Seven Sisters Road. It was mid-afternoon of a perfectly dreadful Sunday, the 18th of September. Watching the sky, Elizabeth was entirely resigned that the sun was about to go out.

Ambrose had avoided looking at her in their conversation up to now. He was a coward, of course. All men were when it came to something like this.

"It may not be permanent," he said at last.

What in the world did *that* mean?

"Would you please stop lying? You know it will."

"I don't know any such thing. I . . . well, I only know what I feel at the moment."

"That you don't love me anymore."

"I never said that!"

"But you mean it. You feel it."

"I don't know what I feel at the moment."

"Well, really, I'm at a loss, then. You just said a moment ago that you're doing this because of your feelings."

"Don't be snide, Elizabeth. It doesn't suit you."

"Funny, that's exactly what Catherine said. Perhaps I'm no longer *me* anymore. Yes, that *is* how I feel. I'm not used to being deceived, you see. I don't know how to respond."

Ambrose suddenly looked ill, but Elizabeth didn't care.

"You love her. Admit it."

"Leave her out of it. She has nothing to do with it."

"Oh, my dearest darling, you really are contemptible! That's the reason you're ending our engagement—the only reason. Why won't you just admit it?"

"We're back there again, are we? I told you I need time to think things over, that's all."

"I see. Do you deny that you're seeing her?"

That day at the Dulwich Picture Gallery, when she had seen Ambrose and . . . *that woman* together, was so vivid in her mind that she felt as though it were branded on her forehead.

"No."

"Well, thank you for that, at least. Please be honest with me, Ambrose, as it will help me to understand what is happening between you and me. What do you find attractive about her?"

"Elizabeth, must we talk about this? I know I'm being hurtful to you. Why do you insist on hurting yourself more?"

"Don't you see, I plan on becoming a saint? The more stigmata I have, the more easily I'll be admitted to Heaven. Is it because she's older and more experienced in matters of love? More exotic and mysterious? Tell me, Ambrose. I seem to have so much to learn."

"Please, Elizabeth. Don't—"

"My goodness, I've been stupid. I'll have to revisit my entire closet to put myself more on display. And I must add all kinds of paints and enamels to my cosmetics tray. Do you think I should use belladonna to make my eyes softer and more seductive?"

He had no time to reply, for Elizabeth, with the sound of a sob in her throat, rose and hurried off in the direction of her home. Just then, the sun came out from behind the clouds, but neither of them noticed.

C

[Scene 2: The drawing room at Nine Columns, the Wilsons' home. It is mid-morning on Wednesday of the following week. Margaret Wilson and her daughter Catherine are sitting together on the settee. The light from the windows is fitful and dull.]

"Nightmares?"

"No, I don't think so, Mother. I believe it's sleepwalking."

Margaret Wilson looked blankly at her daughter. "I hardly believe it's that, Catherine. Have you seen anything? I certainly haven't."

"Yes, mother, I have. Two nights ago, I saw her in the garden."

"Well! Just because she takes a turn in the garden before—"

"It was well after midnight, and she was in her night clothes and barefoot."

"I see. The nights are getting rather cold to be without shoes."

Catherine shook her head with impatience. "Don't be obtuse, Mother. Something is wrong with Elizabeth, and we must get a doctor in to find out what it is."

"Of course, something is wrong. It's her engagement to that foolish Mr. Reed." Mrs. Wilson began rubbing her left thumb energetically over her right fist. "Look at how long it took her to tell me he had thrown her over. That's her way, isn't it? She stews and stews, and before you know it, she'll end up in bed and unable to move." An alarming thought came to her. "Do you think it's brain fever?"

"I think she's deeply unhappy," said Catherine, "and unfortunately, it's manifesting itself in some odd behavior." She didn't want to say the next thing to her mother, but knew she must. "I think she's going outside. At night."

"Outside?"

"Yes—out and about, I mean. On two occasions, I heard something and got up and went to her room. She wasn't there, and her nightgown was on her bed. I'm afraid, you see, that she dressed and left the house."

"And you didn't tell me! . . . Does your father know?"

"No, I haven't said anything to him."

"How awful!" said Mrs. Wilson. "Where do you think she goes?"

Catherine couldn't answer that question, and so didn't try. It was something that worried her greatly, however. They would have to call Dr. Rowse, and perhaps then they would get an answer. For the time being, she would keep to herself the state of Elizabeth's clothes on the mornings after she was gone from her bedroom. Mother didn't need to hear about the dirt on Lizzie's skirts, the briars caught in her sleeves, or the mud on her boots.

℃

[Scene 3: The dining room at the Wilsons' home. It is Monday morning, five days later. Seated at the dining table are Elizabeth, Catherine, Mrs. Margaret Wilson, and her husband, Mr. Hiram Wilson.]

The breakfast table was heartily laden with food and cheerful enough this morning; but the air in the dining room was filled with anger, disappointment, and frustration. To judge by the Wilson family's faces, no one seemed to be enjoying the food, or even tasting it. Perhaps a course of Ambrose Reed Tartare, stuck with four forks, would have lightened the mood at the table.

'I simply don't know what can be done," Margaret Wilson said.

"It's no use repeating yourself, Mother," said Elizabeth, who seemed to seriously resent the plate of food she had been staring at with an angry expression for some time now.

Hiram Wilson, Chairman of the British Railway Department and lord of this particular manor, could hold himself in no longer.

"I'll sue him for alienation of affections!" he announced to the world.

He looked like he could do it, too. He was a thick man of medium height and middle age, with generally the same level of energy and power as the locomotives he oversaw. He wore a beard rather like the one Moses must have worn, and small wire-rimmed glasses that framed eyes like anthracite—the hardest type of coal.

"I believe that's an American term of law, Father," said Catherine Wilson.

"Damn it . . . tortious interference, then, against her! This woman clearly interfered in the marriage contract between Elizabeth and her fiancé," Wilson added, unwilling to pronounce the name of the gentleman who was the other party to the contract.

"That's ridiculous, Hiram," his wife upbraided him. "This isn't a business transaction." A rather subdued "Hmpf!" was the only reply from the other side of the table. Margaret Wilson was perfectly willing to defer to her husband in public and in inconsequential household matters. In fact, she had quite perfected the art; and in society, she was often considered to be 'hardly there'. But she had a good head, which at times could display its own anthracite-like qualities.

She turned to her younger daughter.

"Elizabeth, what was Ambrose's first wife like? We've hardly ever spoken of her."

"I don't know why we should," Elizabeth replied dismissively.

"Well, I should think it might have some bearing if she and Mrs. Bain were alike, don't you?"

"No," replied Elizabeth firmly. "It's absurd. I have no idea what Mrs. Bain is like, except that she appears to be exotic and, oh, I suppose, handsome in a rather severe way."

"And the first wife?"

"All right, Mother, if you must. Her name was Mary Boyle. She was small and dark and secretive-looking, to judge from her photograph. I gather that she was somewhat controlling, and often kept Ambrose feeling at sixes and sevens."

"Well, that's a fault of the man's, isn't it?"

"Mother! I'll not have you speak of Ambrose like that."

"It's true, though, isn't it? And why should you care, my dear? You're not seeing him anymore, are you?"

When Elizabeth didn't reply, Catherine spoke up.

"Yes, she is, Mother. They haven't broken off completely."

"You mean to tell me this blackguard is still seeing my daughter—his jilted fiancée—while courting another woman?" Hiram Wilson fumed, instantly putting his blood pressure at risk. Elizabeth, feeling that she had to stand up for herself, actually defended Ambrose instead:

"He doesn't want to end it entirely, Father. He says he's confused, and needs time to think things out."

"I'll give him confused!" responded Hiram, and somehow everyone knew what he meant.

With that, the bloody affair of breakfast at Nine Columns on the 3rd of October came to a desultory end.

But Margaret Wilson had had an idea. And she meant to act on it.

CHAPTER 13

A Case At Last

s unlikely as a relationship might seem, Mrs. Margaret Wilson and Mr. Julius Pickering, founder of the thriving chain of Pickering Grocers, had one. One could say it was a harmony of opposites.

To begin with, Mrs. Wilson was upper-middle class, in the same way that fish swam in the ocean: it was simply what she *did*. Mr. Pickering, on the other hand, would happily *sell* you a fish, but he simply wasn't of the same school as his friend. Julius Pickering was solidly middle-class, and dressed, spoke, and thought that way. Of course, it was an excellent thing for the British Empire that he and others like him did dress, and speak, and conduct business in the way they did.

Moreover, Mrs. W. and Mr. P. shared an important interest. Both were dedicated to their charitable work on behalf of the destitute. In fact, they shared work on three London charities. These were (1) The Asylum for Fatherless Children (which was located in Finsbury, near where the Wilsons lived); (2) the School for the Indigent Blind, of St. George's Fields in Southwark; and (3) The Home for Consumptive Females, housed in Gloucester Place, Portman Square. Having served on various boards, committees, and benevolent endeavors of each of these charities, the wife of the Chairman of the Railway Department and the founder of a successful grocery chain knew each other quite well.

Julius Pickering (as the reader will recall), was also a founding member of The Society for Supernatural and Psychic Research. It was this fact that had made Margaret Wilson reach out to Pickering a day earlier.

The two friends were having lunch. As to the location, Mrs. Wilson had decided that it was too risky to invite Mr. Pickering to her house—in case Elizabeth somehow got wind of it—and inappropriate for her to visit him at his home. The bar and terrace of the Great Northern Hotel, a railway hotel next to King's Cross station, served her purpose nicely. She was sure that the establishment's nonstop activity would be ideal for disappearing in plain sight.

They were well into the main course and had spoken nothing but pleasantries up until now. It was time for her to broach the reason for her invitation.

"Julius, do you know any hypnotists?"

Pickering paused with his fork halfway to his mouth.

"That's an odd question, Margaret." Mr. Pickering was plainspoken in business, and saw no reason to be otherwise in his personal affairs. "Whatever makes you ask it?"

"I know you're the soul of discretion, Julius. So, I won't beat about the bush. My younger daughter, Elizabeth, is deeply troubled. I'm quite concerned about her, and I believe someone like that may be able to help her."

"I see. I'm very sorry to hear that, Margaret. But wouldn't you prefer a psychiatric doctor? It's quite an accepted specialty now, you know. There's someone I know of, over at St. Bernards—"

Margaret put down her fork.

"Don't be stupid, Julius. You're speaking of Hanwell. I'm not taking my daughter to an asylum. You might just as well tell me I should put her in Bedlam!"

"I meant nothing of the kind. I apologize if it sounded that way. I meant that the doctor could come to you, of course." When Margaret didn't say anything, he added: "What is her principal complaint, if I may ask?"

"She was engaged to be married. And now it's broken off. I'm afraid she's dreadfully distressed over it. Broken-hearted, really."

"I hardly think that a hypnotist—"

"My older daughter, Catherine, says she's sleepwalking."

"Oh, I see. And has that caused trouble in any way?"

"I don't understand."

"Well, has she done anything? Hurt herself . . . or someone else?"

"Of course not!" Margaret said vociferously, then hesitated. "Actually, we really don't know. Catherine says she's sure Elizabeth has been going out at night. Dressed herself and gone out abroad, I mean. Catherine is being very secretive about it all, and I think there's something she isn't telling me."

She sighed deeply. Then she appeared to put what she'd just said aside, as though she'd spent all the time and effort she wanted to on trying to tease apart an impossible knot. She sat up straighter that she had been sitting up until now.

"Julius," she said, with a new note in her voice, "you know, I'm terribly interested in the Society you've been telling me about. Have you any hypnotists on the board?"

Pickering smiled. "I'm afraid it's not like that, Margaret. We're an amateur investigative society. Or, we intend to be at any rate. We're interested in looking into unexplained psychic activity, that kind of thing." He stopped and observed his friend more closely. "Why, you do look unhappy. How can I help, dear?"

Margaret took a long time before she said anything.

"Do you know how some women, who realize they are dying, let their husbands know they want them to marry again?"

"Yes, of course, that's very true."

"Well, what about those women who feel the opposite? Who hate the thought of their about-to-be widowed husband taking another wife?"

"There are those too, I suppose. What are you getting at?"

"I have this odd idea, you see. About Elizabeth's fiancé's first wife."

"Her ex-fiancé, you mean."

"Yes." She put up both hands. "I'm sorry, I'm not making any sense. His name is Ambrose Reed. He's been a widower for three years. Apparently, his first wife was very controlling." She paused, then looked straight at him. "Do you think it's possible, Julius, for someone to exert an influence from beyond the grave?"

He looked at her blankly. "Is that what you're thinking—that this man's dead wife is somehow exercising some influence on your daughter's marriage?"

"You know I've always had an interest in spiritualism. Isn't it possible?"

"And you believe that that's what happening?"

"Will you stop asking me that? I don't *know*! It's all been so sudden and mysterious. The engagement was going along wonderfully. But Ambrose suddenly called it off, as though *something* influenced him. There's an older woman he's been out with socially, but I don't think that's it. I think you and I believe that an influence from the other side can happen. *Does* happen, probably! I would like to try to find out."

She was hugely grateful that Julius didn't scoff, but asked in a serious tone:

"What was her name, the first wife?"

"Mary Boyle. 'Reed,' of course, once she was married: Mrs. Mary Reed."

"What did she die of?"

"Phthisis. Why do you ask?"

"Well, you see, if she were really tubercular, she wouldn't have died suddenly. She'd have known the disease was terminal, and would have had time to get a sense of her husband's intentions about marrying again someday. So, perhaps it's possible."

"Oh, you are wonderful, Julius. You mean that his deceased wife could be interfering somehow? Giving him suggestions, or speaking to him in his sleep, something like that?" She paused, then fairly blurted out: "Or entering my daughter's mind so she begins sleepwalking?"

Julius nearly laughed, but seeing his friend's clear distress, suppressed it. "I haven't the slightest idea," he said, in what he hoped was a kind tone. "Anyway, it would be damned difficult to find out."

"You mean through a séance?"

"Naturally. Maybe more than one. I understand that kind of thing can be quite an undertaking. I have no experience in this, you see."

"Yes, I know that," said Margaret impatiently. "Do you *know* of anyone who can conduct a séance?"

"I do," Julius answered, thinking the matter over even as he spoke. Then that thought cleared and he looked Margaret in the eye.

"And as it happens, my dear, he's a member of the Society."

CHAPTER 14

Séance

jango Pierce-Jones—the person occupying Julius Pickering's thoughts—was otherwise employed at the moment, however. The Commissioner of Police himself, Sir Charles Warren, at his wits' end, had reached out to Pierce-Jones to ask for his help. Scarlet and he had not been the only ones who had noticed the regular monthly intervals in the children's disappearances. Once that fact was recognized, the everyday calendar became an ominous timetable. By the middle of October, anxiety, outrage, and a feeling of helplessness were reaching a crescendo in London.

If the theory of the new moon was correct, they had less than two weeks to apprehend the abductor—and probably, the killer—before he struck again. The next new moon would arrive on October the 16th, and would be present that night and the next. At this point, the police had no leads; and not a trace of any of the children had been found. Pierce-Jones therefore understood keenly why Sir Charles would be reaching out to him as a medium, especially one Scotland Yard had used before.

He, Sir Charles, and Scarlet had discussed their options in the Commissioner's chambers. If any evidence turned up—any object left behind by the kidnapper, or even something touched by him or her that they could identify—Scarlet would lay his hands on it to see if it revealed anything to him.

Scarlet's talents as a psychometrist were officially a secret in the Yard; but he and Pierce-Jones were not naïve enough to think that Sir Charles wasn't privy to everything that went on in the force. But there had been nothing up until this point for Scarlet to make use of. And the scenes of the children's disappearances were so public, with so many lives having crossed and re-crossed the sidewalks and streets and alleys, that visiting them hadn't produced any feelings or visions in him that he could isolate from the chaotic and anonymous energy swirling around in each of them.

Pierce-Jones's talents, on the other hand, could be invaluable where Scarlet's couldn't. His sensibilities and receptiveness made him a master in one environment in particular: as a medium in séances. His ethnic heritage and history—and his past successes—had made him an obvious choice to join The Society for Supernatural and Psychic Research. Now, a frustrated Sir Charles was calling on his skills once more in the context of a police investigation.

The question at hand was a stark and tenuous one: Could someone on The Other Side give them information they couldn't see from here? Another possibility that might emerge from the planned séance was something none of them spoke about, not even to each other. If the children were dead, Pierce-Jones and Scarlet might encounter one or more of their spirits during the session—and perhaps learn a valuable clue about their murderer.

Of course, they were well aware that whatever happened during the séance, word mustn't get out about it. It would seem to be just one more desperate measure on the part of a Scotland Yard that was without suspects. If the séance proved to be successful, well, they would simply keep its occurrence a secret.

As to the possibility of failure, it was simply something they didn't have the luxury to worry about.

The participants were to include Pierce-Jones, Scarlet, and any family members of the missing children who would agree to attend.

That was risky, as it was impossible to predict how a loved one would react if any details of an abduction or murder came through. But they had to take the chance. The sensitivity of a family member—and the willingness of a spirit to seek contact with one of them—were advantages that were simply too great to ignore. Sgt. Jessey would also attend as a necessary security presence.

Two of the children's relatives had agreed to participate. One was Jane Gates, the mother of Sarah Gates, the twelve-year-old who was seen accompanying a shadowy figure on the early evening of 20 July. The other was a surprise. He was Thomas Morrissey, an uncle of Walter Morrissey, the first child to disappear. Walter was a waif with no known relatives in London. But Mr. Morrissey had journeyed to the city from Somerset, determined to do his duty by his family. Scarlet and Pierce-Jones were especially pleased that the Gates woman would be there. Vague as it was, the sighting of an adult (male or female?) with her daughter before she disappeared was the only evidence they had concerning what had happened to the children. Her mother's presence might be a strong enough impetus to compel the child's spirit—if she were there—to reach out.

They met at nine p.m. on Wednesday evening, the 5th of October, in a small sitting room inside the Police Commissioner's chambers. The location was chosen both for the extreme privacy it allowed, and also because it was one of the few rooms at the Yard that didn't have the cold and clinical feel of a large metropolitan police headquarters. The hour was also late enough that the connection might be more easily made, in the absence of the workday bustle and everyday concerns that would occupy the minds of the people in the room. Naturally, time of day made no difference to the dead.

The furniture in the room, its table lamps and pictures on the walls, and a large mirror over the mantlepiece had been removed. Set in their place was a plain card table large enough to accommodate the four simple chairs placed around it. At a few minutes after nine, those present occupied all the seats at the table. Anyone joining after the séance began wouldn't need a chair, of course.

Pierce-Jones gave everyone a moment to relax and settle their breathing. Then he began, without any conventional pleasantries.

"The lights will remain on," he announced. "We won't be proceeding in the dark, so that raps in different places can manifest." The somber and serious quality of his voice was obvious. "The Fox Sisters aren't here this evening. Nor will you be tying me up with rope so that I can free myself within seconds, while the rope's knots rearrange themselves under the table."

If anyone smiled at his wit, it was only inwardly.

"Now, let us please join hands." Mrs. Gates was on Pierce-Jones's right; to her right Scarlet sat; and next to him, Mr. Morrissey, who grasped the medium's left hand. "The spiritual circuit is now complete," Pierce-Jones informed them. "Let us bow our heads."

They did so.

"We are here tonight to seek knowledge and help in the search for the beloved lost children. We will be reaching out to The Other Side, in the hope that someone who has gone before will wish to communicate with us." Deliberately, he did not mention that any of the missing children might be among that group.

He knew that what he said next might surprise the two children's relatives sitting at the table.

"We ask this help in the name of God and all that is holy."

He let that last statement sit for a moment. He knew the Church's disapproval of a sitting like this, and any attempts to contact those in the afterlife. But he was of the camp that viewed all of God's mysteries as part of His grace. And, of course, he was well aware of the Bible's story of King Saul summoning the departed spirit of Samuel in the underworld through the Witch of Endor.

"Let us sing the hymn, *Sun of My Soul*," said Pierce-Jones, "to help in our task tonight and to protect us." And the five of them—including Sgt. Jessey who stood as unobtrusively as possible in a corner of the room—softly sang the hymn they all knew well:

Sun of my soul, Thou Saviour dear,
It is not night if Thou be near:
O may no earth-born cloud arise
To hide Thee from Thy servant's eyes.
When the soft dews of kindly sleep
My wearied eyelids gently steep,
Be my last thought, how sweet to rest
For ever on my Saviour's breast.
Abide with me from morn till eve,
For without Thee I cannot live;
Abide with me when night is nigh,
For without Thee I dare not die.
If some poor wand'ring child of Thine
Have spurn'd to-day the voice Divine,
Now, Lord, the gracious work begin;
Let him no more lie down in sin.
Watch by the sick; enrich the poor
With blessings from Thy boundless store;
Be every mourner's sleep to-night
Like infant's slumbers, pure and light.
Come near and bless us when we wake,
Ere through the world our way we take;
Till in the ocean of Thy love
We lose ourselves in Heav'n above.

As they raised their heads after the hymn was finished, the medium looked at each of them in turn and said, "Thank you."

"And thank you for doing this, Mr. Pierce-Jones," said Thomas Morrissey, in a deep voice. "May God bless you."

Pierce-Jones waited a moment, then said: "I would like to prepare you for what to expect tonight. If we are successful, we should experience something very different from what you may have heard or read about.

"We are conducting a search to find someone on the other side of the veil who will speak to us, and many times nothing happens. We seek contact with a spirit who agrees to serve as a 'control,' that is, a medium in the spirit world. This entity, if we find one, will try to communicate with me as the medium in our world.

"The control will pass on what anyone who approaches him or her wants to say to us. But it is not always easy for these departed spirits to express themselves clearly. Those who are new to the Other Side have the greatest difficulty. If we find someone, that spirit will share his or her thoughts with the control, who will then try to impress those thoughts on my inner mind. If I am able to receive them, I will then try to put them into words. What you hear me say aloud will be those thoughts, filtered through both the control and my own interpretation of what is being said. There are many opportunities for error."

Sarah Gates, the mother of the missing girl, said: "Will you go into a trance?"

"Yes, I am a trance medium. But I will speak in my own voice, or what is called a direct voice and not a trance voice. Even the definitions, you see, do not always apply. I am told my voice becomes somewhat hollow. You will hear the difference clearly when contact is made."

Thomas Morrissey: "Will the . . . spirit speaking to us tell us their name?"

"Likely, not," came the reply. "Names are very difficult for the departed to convey, since they represent a concept and are not solid things. Sometimes a spirit will try to build up the first letter of their name, and that may help us. But pet family names and nicknames are sometimes used, which can be confusing if the person who would recognize it is not at the sitting."

He waited for any other questions, but there were none. He looked across the table and said: "Dr. Scarlet, are you ready? You will break the circuit and bring me out if necessary?"

"I am, and I will. Good luck."

"We'll begin now," said Pierce-Jones. "I will close my eyes, but it's not necessary for any of you to do so. Try to calm and center yourself inwardly. Place your feet flat on the floor, and breathe deeply. Open the gate of your mind to accept whatever presents itself tonight."

He cleared his throat once. He remained silent for what seemed a very long time. Then he said in his normal voice, loudly and clearly, but without inflection:

"We reach out to the Other Side tonight, seeking help to find the lost children. Who is there to help us? Will someone act as a guide for anyone who wants to speak? Are there others near who want to speak through you? Will you help them do so?"

Silence.

"There are two here tonight especially who humbly ask for your help. Jane, who is grieving because of the disappearance of her daughter, Sarah; and Thomas, who seeks any information on his nephew, Walter. If someone there knows anything about these children or the other children who have recently disappeared, please come to us now. Spirit guide, is anyone there to speak to us?"

Silence.

"Are *you* there, to help anyone who is gathering near you now?"

Nothing.

"Has someone come? Are there those who wish to speak through you to us?"

Again, only a long silence. Pierce-Jones continued, undeterred by the lack of response.

"Jane and Thomas are asking for the sake of their loved ones, Sarah and Walter." He took a breath to say something else, but stopped. His face went blank, with all its expression removed, as if, in fact, his mind had suddenly become neutral and wholly receptive. When he spoke, his voice—though it seemed impossible—sounded hollow, as if he was speaking in a large chamber:

"M— M— M— Mi— Miriam. Miriam is here and wants to help. She sees others around her who wish to speak, who came here before

the time you are speaking of. They are ready now to make contact."

Pierce-Jones answered in his new hollow voice:

"Who are they, and what do they want to say? Can they speak through you?"

"I thought you said names were too difficult," Morrissey objected.

"Be quiet!" Scarlet scolded him sharply. "Spirit controls have usually been there a very long time, and have mastered conveying names. This one seems to be speaking of herself in the third person. Some do. Now be quiet."

"We seek information only on the children who have disappeared in London recently."

'Recently' meant nothing to the spirit guide and any others gathered there, of course. But Pierce-Jones didn't know how else to convey their needs.

"Can anyone there help us? Does anyone know Jane's daughter Sarah, or Thomas's nephew Walter, or any of the others who have disappeared? Can they see any of those children on our side? Do they know where the children are? Will you help them speak?"

"They know their children, they are telling Miriam, and want to speak to them. Will you—"

But Pierce-Jones was insistent.

"No, it is not their children we are asking about. We are trying—"

"There are too many here, and they all want to speak! It is too difficult. Some can manifest themselves, but others cannot. There is always something rising from the earth plane, which they can see and understand. All can see and understand. But the ones who are newly here cannot build up anything in their minds to convey to me. Others—"

Again, Pierce-Jones persisted.

"Only the London children who have disappeared" . . . He struggled with the concept . . . **"In the now in our time. Are there any there who know them?"**

A long silence intervened. Then:

"There is someone here . . . someone is coming. A woman. She knows these children. Miriam will ask her if she wants to speak.

". . . No, she is not good. She takes the Life-Force! She doesn't give, doesn't love. She is a stranger to me. I cannot tell— Miriam feels her anger.

"Now, she is telling me that the children are here. There will be more, she says. . . Oh, Miriam is frightened!"

"For God's sake!" screamed Jane Gates. "Is my daughter there?"

"Yes! She says the children are on this side. But they are not here with us. She says she has them. But she is a taker of the Life-Force. . . . She is going away now."

Jane Gates: "Oh, my God! Sarah!"

"Is there anyone else there who can speak! Can you help them speak?"

"Many are here, but no one knows of what you are asking. . . .

Wait. There is another near me who wants to speak. This one is good. She said she knows who the other one is. I am . . . she is trying to impress her thoughts on my mind. But it is difficult—she hasn't been here long enough."

"Help her speak!"

Then things became chaotic fast. Mrs. Gates had fallen forward with her head on the table, sobbing uncontrollably. Pierce-Jones on her left, and Scarlet on her right, were struggling to keep holding hands with her as she thrashed and moaned. Thomas Morrissey sat still as a statue, his eyes colorless, his face white as plaster; and his hands holding the two other men's hands were cold.

Suddenly, from out of the center of the table, blood began to bubble up from some invisible source—a small fountain of red that spread across the table until it flowed off every side. Everyone's sleeves became wet where their arms rested on the table. The blood began to spread on the floor. They heard a sound from underneath the table, and all of them looked there.

A large snake, easily eight feet long, was slithering around the legs of the table and in and out through the participants' legs. But the men's grips held firm, and the spiritual circuit did not break.

"KILL THE SERPENT!"

. . . someone on the Other Side said, in Pierce-Jones's hollow voice. And then:

"AMBROSE! AMBROSE!"

"Who the devil is Ambrose?" Scarlet said out loud before a sound like a giant waterfall filled the room, and for every person present, everything went black.

CHAPTER 15

Terra Incognita

carlet opened his eyes on a sitting room in Scotland Yard that was impossibly and inexplicably *normal.* As he watched, the others' eyes opened—Pierce-Jones, then Jane Gates, and finally Thomas Morrissey—all of them looking around with the same confused expression he was sure was on his face.

They all saw a mostly empty room in the Police Commissioner's chambers in which the furnishings had been removed, and the small card table at which they sat put in their place. The table and the floor were dry; the room was silent and still. They could hear horses' hooves striking the pavement in the street below, and occasionally the creaking of a carriage's running gear, but that was all. No snake slithered on the floor around their feet.

That something extraordinary had happened was clear to all of them. That they were dealing with a powerful—and perhaps dangerous—conjured spirit was a thought that only Scarlet and Pierce-Jones shared, however. Jane Gates and Thomas Morrissey, the missing children's relatives, would not have known how séances typically unfolded. But Scarlet and Pierce-Jones knew. The intrusion of a malevolent spirit; the fear felt by the spirit control; the visual hallucinations; and finally, the name of someone who was not present called out, and for an unknown reason—all these things were unanticipated. Scarlet realized that they were in undiscovered territory, and he knew that Pierce-Jones would feel the same.

The sitting had also produced some half-expected—and dreaded—news. The missing children were dead. Miriam, the spirit control, had said, *"She is telling me that the children are here."* Meaning on The Other Side. And, more ominously: *"There will be more."*

Miriam had said 'she.' But who could that be? A relative of the children who had already passed? No, that wasn't it, thought Scarlet. The control had also said *"She is not good."* And more ominous still: *"She takes the Life-Force, doesn't give, doesn't love."*

Was the malevolent entity that had appeared during the séance connected with the children in any way? How was that possible? Whatever it was, it dwelt on the Other Side, not here. But Miriam had also said, *"She knows these children."* Does 'she' know who abducted and killed them—and does she want to give them information now?

In Scarlet's mind, the fact that Miriam said this entity 'is not good' didn't mean that that entity had harmed the children herself. It was said that in the afterlife, the newly deceased were placed on the appropriate level based on the lives they had led. Then, as their souls learned and were purified, they ascended to higher levels, a process that took the equivalent of many human lifetimes. Was this unknown spirit's offer of help part of that purification process?

These thoughts had occurred in rapid succession in Scarlet's mind. Now he set them aside. The children's relatives required his attention. After all, they had just learned that their daughter and nephew had been murdered, and they needed any support he could offer.

He called to Sergeant Jessey, who came forward, looking as unsettled as any of them. Jane Gates was still sobbing, and Morrissey was speaking to her softly. The man was doing his best to play the strong and stoic Englishman, but his lower lip was quivering. Scarlet and Pierce-Jones rose from the table, saying what they could to soothe and comfort the relatives of the slain children, as they now knew them to be. It did little good, of course. But at last Jessey was able to lead the relatives from the room, and the two of them were alone.

Pierce-Jones's features were dark and drawn in—his forehead now creased by two vertical lines that hadn't been there before; and his eyes appeared focused intently on something that wasn't in the room. Scarlet waited until the far-away look left the eyes, then said:

"What d'you make of it?"

Django Pierce-Jones shook his head. "An odd business," he said. "I've never encountered anything like it before. Terrifying, really. Visual hallucinations . . . perhaps auditory ones, too. But from where?"

"Or whom?"

"Exactly. . . . There was another entity present at the end, wasn't there?"

Scarlet nodded and said, "The one Miriam said was good."

"That's right. And again, Miriam said 'she'—so there had to be *two* female entities present, one after the other." And then: "Were they both there at the end? And if so, which of them yelled a warning about the snake . . . or 'serpent,' as she called it?"

"I couldn't tell from your voice," said Scarlet. "And then you shouted 'Ambrose!' immediately afterwards."

They lapsed into silence. Another realization had come to them during the séance, which they hadn't spoken of yet. But it was grim and frightening and had to be voiced. Scarlet did so now.

"We have a killer of children on our hands."

They were on their way out of the building when a young constable strode up and handed Scarlet an envelope.

"For you, sir. Delivered yesterday, as I understand it. But we was told you had important business on hand and we was not to disturb you."

Scarlet thanked the man and removed the contents. It consisted of two handwritten pages, on business notepaper. He glanced quickly at the letterhead on the first page, said: "It's from Pickering," then read the contents.

"I'll be damned," he proclaimed, then handed the two sheets of paper over. Django read the following:

4 October 1887

Dear Mr. Scarlet,
I trust this finds you well. I'm writing on rather a delicate matter, which I hope that you and Mr. Pierce-Jones can help me resolve.

Today, I dined with an associate in my charitable work who presented me with a peculiar request. In sum, her daughter is in a perilous mental state over an engagement recently called off by the young gentleman involved, who is a widower of some three years.

My friend has the extraordinary idea that the man's dead wife is interfering in the relationship between her widower husband (the young gentleman) and my friend's daughter. Do you know of such documented occurrences? No doubt this extraordinary proposition of control exercised from beyond the grave provides precisely the type of occurrence the Society has been looking for. If such a thing is actually taking place, however, the question becomes, "How the devil do you prove it?"

Mrs. Margaret Wilson—my friend—is convinced that a séance is in order, to try to contact the spirit of the dead wife (her name was Mrs. Mary Reed) and get to the bottom of it. Apparently, she was something of a mysterious figure and rather controlling of her husband when alive, which perhaps makes this idea more plausible. Is all of this a wild notion, or is it a phenomenon you've heard about before?

I am anxious to learn if this is something you can help with. I'm thinking in particular of Mr. Pierce-Jones and his undoubted talents in séances, and whether you might speak to him. I thought it appropriate to write to you, given your own abilities, and also because I wasn't certain if the Society's Secretary should initiate an investigation. At any rate, do you think he would agree to hold one, or convene one, or however it's thought of?

I feel that time is of the essence, as the daughter — whose name is Elizabeth Wilson, by the way — is disturbed, as evidenced by her recent sleepwalking. Kindly reply at your earliest.

Your friend,
Julius Pickering

P.S. The former fiancé's name--the young widower — is Ambrose Reed.

Django looked up from the letter. "Well, one thing seems likely," he said, though he looked more puzzled than sure.

"We've found our Ambrose," Scarlet finished the thought for him.

CHAPTER 16

A Fevered Visit

he next morning, the 6th of October—a Thursday—Dr. William Scarlet and Django Pierce-Jones sat in the front parlour of Ambrose Reed's home on Bayswater Road in London. They had waited long enough to be able to watch the sunlight move across the wallpaper on the wall opposite them.

Had they noticed the sky last night, they would have seen a waning gibbous moon. But it was the coming new moon they were interested in. That would arrive in exactly ten days and last for two nights, October 16th and 17th.

Last evening's séance, however chaotic and confusing at the end, had produced one tangible clue—the one they were following up on now. Through the spirit control Miriam and in Django's voice, someone on the Other Side had shouted the name 'Ambrose.' From Pickering's letter of two days ago, they had learned that that was the name of the fiancé of Pickering's friend's daughter, Elizabeth. That young woman was in distress over her troubled engagement to a Mr. Ambrose Reed. It seemed to be far too much of a coincidence that the name 'Ambrose' from their sitting was linked to *another* séance being planned to investigate possible recent occult behavior.

Was there a connection between the two? What did one series of events—the abductions and murders—have to do with the abrupt and unlikely behavior of both the widower Ambrose Reed and that of his fiancée, Elizabeth Wilson, including her sleepwalking?

Most puzzling—and perhaps most important—why had two different entities in the afterlife linked Pierce-Jones's questions to the murdered children and the name Ambrose?

These were the questions occupying Scarlet's mind as he sat in the parlour of Ambrose Reed's house when an elderly, well-dressed gentleman entered the room. The tall and frail-looking man carried a tell-tale physician's bag in his right hand. He walked straight up to Scarlet, transferred the bag to his left hand and shook Scarlet's hand rather weakly.

"Mr. Scarlet? I am Francis Milkwater, attending on Mr. Reed. I'm afraid he's been ill, perhaps you had not heard? I have no objection to his receiving visitors, however. He's doing well today, more or less."

"How do you do? What is his ailment, Mr. Milkwater?"

"Brain fever," answered the older man without hesitation. "Mr. Reed has been under considerable strain lately, and I'm afraid it's progressed to that." He looked down and shook his head. "We're never called in good time, are we, Mr. Scarlet? I'd have been able to stave this off, more or less, but there you have it. It's brain fever now."

"And what have you prescribed, sir?"

"Oh, the usual: wet sheets, and hot and cold baths. Plenty of rest, of course. And above all, avoiding any emotional upset until the brain's inflammation begins to subside."

"I see. Am I correct in thinking this has something to do with the recent cancellation of Mr. Reed's engagement?"

"You'd have to ask him that. Have you spoken to the family?"

"I've spoken with his fiancée—or former fiancée, I suppose I should say."

It was true that Scarlet had done that, if briefly. It was probably more accurate, however, to say that it was the young woman's mother, Mrs. Wilson, who had advocated that he speak with Mr.

Ambrose Reed. The daughter, Elizabeth, had agreed to that plan with no great conviction. She had, however, suggested that Scarlet and Pierce-Jones send a note to Ambrose introducing themselves first, which they had done.

"Well, if it's all right with them, it's certainly not my place to stand in the way," said the older physician. "Mr. Reed hasn't been a frequent patient of mine, though I know his family." He cast a glance at Pierce-Jones, seemed about to say something, but let it go. "Just don't tax him for too long, will you?"

"Indeed, I won't," replied Scarlet. "Thank you, Dr. Milkwater, for your kindness."

The old man nodded emphatically once, and was gone.

Only now did Scarlet notice the manservant, who had moved from the hall's shadows into the doorway of the parlour.

"If you gentlemen will come this way," the servant said, and the two of them followed him up the stairs.

Ambrose Reed was sitting up in bed, his hands gently clasped on the coverlet before him. A visitor's first impression was that he was remarkably handsome. In fact, thought Scarlet, he *looked* the part of the young artist to perfection. He had a high forehead with thinning brown hair above it, and well-formed brows and eyes below that. His nose was straight, with a classic look. The mouth was small, and held placidly closed at the moment. The chin was in proportion to the mouth, though it rose up slightly at the end. His side-whiskers were rather long and ended below the ears. Had he been strong enough to work at the moment, he might have painted himself just like this: a Romantic hero at a time of illness. To Scarlet's practiced eye, the man was flushed and enervated.

He gazed at his two visitors now with a look that seemed equal parts expectation and boredom. Clearly, Scarlet thought, it was incumbent upon him as a visitor to the sick room to speak.

"Please forgive our intrusion, Mr. Reed. I am William Scarlet, and this is my associate, Django Pierce-Jones." The next part had puzzled him, as he believed that mentioning the Society for

Supernatural and Psychic Research would be a mistake at this early stage. "I am a doctor. Mrs. Margaret Wilson asked if I might pay you a visit. I've just spoken to Dr. Milkwater downstairs, who has agreed—as far as your health is concerned—that I might talk with you."

"And my other visitor?" asked Reed in a rather soft, quiet voice. "Is he here to hypnotize me? Or perhaps we shall have a séance?"

"I see you are well informed as to who we are," said Scarlet evenly, then added: "Splendid!" while gesturing with his palms held upward. "We can get to the point, then. Please understand, Mr. Reed, we have no intention of prying into your private affairs. We would simply like to understand why your name arose in an investigation we are conducting. As you may already know, I am employed as a surgeon with the Metropolitan Police. We are investigating—"

"The cases of the children who have disappeared, I would imagine. It's not a difficult guess, Mr. Scarlet."

"Yes, of course. You're quite right."

"Though frankly, I can't understand why you're here. You say my name was mentioned in your investigation? By whom, and in what sense?"

Here, Pierce-Jones naturally stepped in.

"I was conducting a séance, Mr. Reed. I'm not at liberty to say who attended the sitting. But a connection was successfully made with spirits on the Other Side, one of whom shouted your name."

Pierce-Jones had chosen this blunt description deliberately. But if he expected a shocked reaction, the man in the bed didn't give him one.

"Really? You mean a spirit from the other side, as you call it, suddenly yelled out 'Ambrose Reed!' and nothing else? How very extraordinary!"

"Your first name, only," replied Pierce-Jones. "And yes, nothing else."

"I must say it's quite wonderful," said Reed. "Let's write a play around the incident and put it on the stage at the first opportunity!"

Reed was getting more flushed. Thinking about the man's blood pressure, Scarlet made his voice more soothing.

"I'm afraid we're in the dark, Mr. Reed." Poor choice of words or not, he went on: "Can you think of any reason why your name should come up in this particular aspect of our investigation?"

"Don't be ridiculous. There must be scores of men named Ambrose in London. Perhaps hundreds."

"I'm sure there are," Scarlet responded. "Perhaps we are wasting our time . . . and yours, of course." He decided to try a different approach. He thought he might have overexcited Reed unnecessarily. The man had lain back on the pillow and looked tired.

"I would like you to know, sir, that as a doctor, I am at your service in terms of any help I might offer with your care. I understand you have been under considerable strain due to your personal affairs."

Ambrose said wearily: "Let's be frank, shall we, Mr. Scarlet? My engagement is off. Elizabeth and I are still seeing each other, if you must know. There . . . you are now thoroughly brought up to date."

But Scarlet wasn't about to give ground. "If I may ask, the young lady has also been ill, is that correct?"

"Broken engagements tend towards such results," said Reed tonelessly.

It was a delicate moment. Scarlet was certain that Django wanted to question Reed as well, but thankfully was maintaining his silence. Even if the conversation was strained, a dialogue had opened up between Reed and him, and he wanted to keep it going.

"If I may ask, sir," he continued, "did it ever occur to you that both you and your ex-fiancée becoming . . . incapacitated at the same time was unusual?"

"Well, it's obvious what's happening, isn't it, Mr. Scarlet? My dearly departed wife, Mary, is angry that I've rushed into another relationship *after only three years*, and is making sure my engagement ends up in the dust yard. She probably wandered into *your* séance by accident, having taken a wrong turning somewhere."

Despite Reed's uncanny approach to the substance of Pickering's letter, Scarlet said, in a neutral tone of voice:

"You don't believe such a thing is possible, then?"

"How in God's name would I know! . . . Mr. Pierce-Jones, what's your expert opinion?" When he got no answer, Reed sighed deeply and said, "I'm sorry, gentlemen. I'm tired. But I really don't know how to help you."

"It is we who must apologize, Mr. Reed. We've taxed you, and you clearly need your rest. Thank you for your time."

As the two men were leaving, Scarlet noticed a framed photograph on the mantlepiece between where he was standing and the door. From the Wilsons' description, this must be Reed's deceased wife, Mary. The picture showed a dark, petite woman with a mass of tight black curls that reached past her shoulders. She was sitting in front of a photographer's forest backdrop, dressed in a black dress with flowing skirts, and looking down demurely. She had round, regular features, and her mouth seemed to carry the hint of a smile.

He absent-mindedly picked up the framed photo as he said, "And is this your wife?"

He didn't hear what the other man answered. He felt the familiar inward blow, and the room immediately fell away. His hand still held out the framed photograph toward Reed, but his gaze shifted so he was looking straight ahead. He was staring at something else now, with the far-away look in his eyes that betrayed the fact that he was experiencing a vision. Django noticed it at once, and quickly looked over at Reed. But the man seemed not to notice—he was looking at Scarlet as if he expected the physician to go on after he'd answered a curt "Yes" to Scarlet's question. Now, a slightly quizzical look was coming into his eyes.

Django crossed quickly and took the framed photo from Scarlet's unresisting hand. He glanced at it briefly and said to Reed in a covering voice, if the man in the bed had been sharp enough to notice Scarlet's behavior.

"A striking woman! I wonder if she had any Romani blood, like me. Her hair and some of her features seem to indicate it. Do you know by any chance if she did?"

Reed transferred his gaze to Pierce-Jones. "There was some mention of it from time to time. But I don't know that she ever looked into it seriously."

Both men paused, each, perhaps, wondering what he might say to cover the silence.

"It is an interesting theory," Scarlet's voice broke in. "I've always felt that if our ancestral roots were examined closely, we'd find many more connections than we ever imagined."

It gave Django the opportunity to put the framed photograph back on the mantlepiece. The two of them nodded politely to the bedridden man and exited the room. Only when they'd walked down the front steps of the house and were a good way down the Bayswater Road, did Pierce-Jones turn to Scarlet.

"What did you see?"

The other looked inward, remembering.

"At first, I didn't see anything so much as *feel*," he said. "That was different for me, and it's hard to describe. I didn't feel evil from the photograph, though evil was present somehow. I can't really explain it. I sensed that there were two entities present: one good, the other very bad. I don't know how I knew that, just that I did."

"Male or female?"

"I couldn't tell. The evil one was very angry, though, and I felt tremendous power. The other was strong too, but quiet and patient. And I had the odd feeling that I wasn't just observing, but that I was involved somehow. Don't ask me how that's possible—I don't know."

"Were either of them trying to reach out to you?"

"One of them was, I think. The other was holding her back."

"Ah!"

"What is it?"

"You said 'her.' So at least one of them was female."

"Yes, you're right!" Scarlet agreed, realizing it now. But then he shook his head. "As to the second entity, I have no idea whether it was male or female." He tried visualizing what he saw again. "No, it's no good."

He suddenly stopped walking and took his friend's arm. He looked at the taller man intently.

"And then, Django, I saw the children. Their faces appeared—all of them—but they were whisked away immediately and there came a feeling of . . . possession. As if someone *took them back again.* It was then that I came to, and heard Reed answer your question. That's how quickly all of it happened."

They began walking once more. Pierce-Jones let some time pass before he spoke again.

"And do you think it's all a coincidence—your touching that photograph in Reed's bedroom and seeing the children?"

"Like bloody hell," answered Scarlet.

CHAPTER 17

The Mystery Woman

William Scarlet, M.D. now faced two dilemmas. First was the implacable calendar. There were only ten days until October 16th and the new moon. The second was Sir Edward Mallinson, Chief Surgeon of the Metropolitan Police and Scarlet's superior. At best, Sir Edward would frown upon the methods Scarlet and Pierce-Jones were now employing in the missing children case. If he found out about them, he could shut down their line of inquiry entirely, despite the Commissioner's interest. Sir Charles need never find out why his Chief Surgeon had decided to pull Dr. Scarlet off the case.

Scarlet and Pierce-Jones, of course, had only one tenuous lead regarding the murdered children—and to be honest, it was hardly even that. The connection between the entities who appeared during the séance revealing the fate of the children, and the recent domestic disturbances of a respectable family, was fragile indeed. The fact that those entities had been present at both the séance and Scarlet's vision in Reed's bedroom was, for the moment, simply puzzling. It wasn't anything that would stand up in any official inquiry of the children's deaths.

At this point, the two members of the Society seemed to be facing an opening into a dark and tantalizing wood. To go forward in any direction, they would have to step very carefully.

Their next move was, however, an obvious one in terms of police procedure. For that Scarlet was thankful. They needed to set up surveillance on their sole suspect, Reed. The difficulty was how to do so without Mallinson finding out about it. The option of Scarlet explaining to his superior that he was proceeding in a multiple murder case based on a) a strange and inexplicable séance, and b) one of his visions of the very type that Mallinson loathed and had in fact forbidden was out of the question.

Reed must be watched, that much was clear. But it had to be done in secret as far as Scotland Yard's knowledge and records were concerned.

Fortunately, the man was bedridden at the moment and they wouldn't be forced to chase him all over London during a lively social calendar. To begin with, they must simply keep a watch on Reed's house in Bayswater Road, observing who came to visit and how much time each person spent there.

Sgt. Jessey and PC Henry Simms 237D, a young policeman Jessey was fond of and who could be trusted, would provide the manpower they needed. The two men would watch the house on their individual off-shifts, whenever those were scheduled: one man from 8.00 a.m. until just before 4.00 p.m. when the shifts at the Yard changed; the other from that time until 11.00 p.m. The small hours of the morning were deemed unlikely enough where visitors were concerned that they needn't be covered. The men's wives were enlisted to prepare double sets of sandwiches: one for their husbands' official shifts, and another for their plainclothes volunteer duty.

In the event, it became an interesting peek into the life of a rising young artist in the *demimonde* of the London art scene. The list of visitors to Bayswater Road that the policemen created looked like this:

SERGEANT JESSEY'S LOG

Friday, 7 October

8.00 a.m. Maid takes in milk from top step. Punctual!
9.18 Mr. Milkwater (doctor) arr.
9.42 Milkwater lv.
10.05 Butcher's boy arr. (back door)
10.25 BB Lv. (flirting w/ maid?)
10.36 Postman
10.50 Grocer's delivery (back door)
10.56 Grocer Lv.
11.10 Butler (name?) Lv. w/letters
11.45 Butler rtn.
12.03 p.m. Elderly dandy arr. by cab
1.37 Same leaves
3.00 Middle-aged lady arr. by cab (Who??)

Sgt. Jessey's notations (with one or two exceptions where he'd included a personal comment) were as mundane and uninteresting as most such surveillance notes. Scarlet suspected that the 'elderly dandy' who arrived at noon was an art dealer. The second unknown visitor was more tantalizing, as it described a 'middle-aged lady' who arrived at the house at 3.00 p.m., and hadn't left by the time Jessey ended his shift.

PC Simms started his log at 4.13 p.m., apparently having been slightly delayed in arriving at the scene of his assignment.

PC SIMMS'S LOG

Fri., 7 Oct.
4.13 PM Arrived. Begin shift.
4.27 PM Postman arrives with afternoon post.
5.05 PM Messenger arrives. Maid answers door, takes envelope.
6.00 PM One male, two females arrive. by cab. Young,

fashionably dressed. Friends of Reed?
8.22 PM Cab draws up, three friends(?) leave.
9.00 PM Young male arrives on foot from East on Bayswater Road. Met by maid or kitchen maid at back door. They step into alley at back of house. Can't observe behaviour.
9.20 PM Maid re-enters back door of house, putting pins in hair. Male visitor leaves same time, walking East on Bayswater Road.
11.00 PM End of shift.

Arrangements had been made for Pierce-Jones to meet with Sgt. Jessey at 4.00 p.m. to discuss his observations, and Scarlet with PC Simms at 11.00 p.m. to do the same. Now Scarlet examined the results. There were two items that held interest for them: one in Jessey's log, and the other among Simms's entries.

The "middle-aged woman" who arrived by cab at 3.00 p.m. on Sgt. Jessey's shift, wasn't observed leaving by Simms. Apparently, either she was still in the house, or had left in the hours after 11.00 p.m., when their surveillance ended until the following morning. Jessey hadn't been able to give Pierce-Jones any further information, as all the sergeant saw was the arrival by cab of the woman, and her quick entrance into the house.

The visit by the three 'friends' from 6.00 to 8.22 was the only item of interest in Simms's log. Scarlet questioned the man about it now.

"Did you notice anything about their mood?"

"Beg pardon, sir?"

"When they arrived, did they appear serious? Or did it seem to be more of a social visit? Were they relaxed and chatting with one another, for instance?"

"Yes, chatting. A social visit, I'd say."

"And when they left . . . any change of mood?"

"Not that I noticed, sir. They seemed the same as when they went in. Silly, like."

Scarlet decided the trio was probably just what they looked like: friends of Reed's from the artist's community, on a visit to a sick friend. The only other interesting aspect of the two logs was that, despite his illness, Reed was able to receive—and presumably entertain—a possible art dealer and three presumed friends.

The romantic intrigue between the maid and her young man (the butcher's boy?) was what one would find in any house with servants. He was sure it meant nothing. His mind returned to the visit of the middle-aged woman.

Who was she? It was damnably frustrating not to know what went on *inside* the house! How interesting it would be, he thought now, if the Metropolitan Police could openly employ him and Django in cases like this that included a supernatural element. They'd have all of the Yard's resources at their disposal, instead of patching together a clandestine operation like this one. But the follow-up thought came instantly: *over Mallinson's dead body!*

He thanked Simms for his yeoman's service last night, reminding him to be in place again tomorrow at 4.00 p.m. sharp. The next day was Saturday—well, it was after midnight now, so it was already Saturday. Scarlet expected some slight change in the schedule of visitors to the house on the first day of the weekend. Tradesmen's visits should be fewer, for instance, though Reed might have more social visitors. As it happened, that was only half-true.

Sgt. Jessey's Saturday log included these entries:

SERGEANT JESSEY'S LOG, DAY TWO

Saturday, 8 October
7.47 a.m. Milkman. (late bc Sat.?)
8.05 Nurse arr. by cab.
8.15 Mr. Milkwater lv. Hails cab.
8.25 Dustman arrives. Discussion at
front door, butler shaking
head. Pays man. Dustman lvs.

9.07 Eliz. Wilson arr. by cab. Hurried.
9.40 Cobbler arr. w/ men's boots.
10.00 Kitchen(?) maid Lv.
10.22 Postman
11.10 Same maid ret. w/ groceries.

Simms's log looked like this:

PC SIMMS'S LOG, DAY TWO

Sat., 8 Oct.
3.50 PM Arrived at post.
4.01 PM Nurse arrives by cab from Eastern direction.
4.12 PM Different nurse leaves, hails Cab, proceeds West.
6.00 PM Miss Elizabeth Wilson(?) leaves. Hails cab, proceeds North.
6.30 PM Lady in black cape and hood arrives. Didn't see cab. Let in quickly.
7.30 PM Same(?) woman in hood leaves. Walks quickly East on Craven Terrace.
9.14 PM Lights out in house.

Looking over the two logs that night after Simms's shift ended, Scarlet immediately saw what Django had pointed out to him earlier in the day concerning Sgt. Jessey's notes. Far from being the mundane entries of the previous day, both of today's logs contained essential information, while departing radically from the previous day's observed activities at the house.

Early Saturday morning, for instance, had been particularly busy at the Reed residence, even hectic. Scarlet had been mistaken about less tradesmen's activity, but that didn't matter. Some of the other things Sgt. Jessey had noted, however, seemed to be of considerable importance. In fact, if you looked carefully, *all* of them were.

At 8.05, someone who appeared to be a private nurse had arrived. Ten minutes later, Dr. Milkwater *left*. That meant he had arrived at the house at some earlier time that morning (the two policemen weren't covering the 11.00 p.m. – 8.00 a.m. time period, so the exact time wasn't known). While there, he had presumably summoned the nurse who arrived just after eight. Ten minutes after the physician's departure, a dustman—probably there to clean out the boiler—was turned away after being paid. Shortly after *that*, Elizabeth Wilson arrived, in a hurried state. Jessey's last entry noted a maid leaving the house, and returning an hour later with groceries.

What it added up to was this: Reed must have become worse during the night, necessitating a wee hours' visit from Dr. Milkwater and the hiring of a full-time nurse. Elizabeth Wilson must have been informed as well. She had arrived at the house at 9.00 and hadn't left by the time Jessey finished his shift.

Of further significance: A dustman had been turned away (though paid) from what was presumably an appointment to carry on with some work at the house. Also, rather than order any necessary groceries to be delivered, the maid had gone out for them herself.

PC Simms's log continued the tale of a house in disorder. An exchange of private nurses on duty at the house had occurred at 4.00 p.m., coinciding with the start of the young policeman's shift. (He had arrived ten minutes early, presumably to make up for his tardiness the day before.) Two hours later, Elizabeth Wilson left— meaning that she had been at the house for nine hours. Exactly thirty minutes after that, at six-thirty p.m., someone wearing a cape and hood arrived on foot, without having been let out at the address from a cab.

Scarlet was convinced that both the careful arrival and the anonymity of the outfit were deliberate—and that this person was the mysterious woman who had visited the previous day. That she arrived a half-hour (to the minute) after Elizabeth had left was also suggestive, as was the fact that this time she only stayed an hour. All of it pointed to a secretive meeting that the woman—or Reed, or both—didn't want to be known.

They had better find out who this Mystery Woman was.

CHAPTER 18

A Sister's Concern

"May I help you, Dr. Scarlet?"

Catherine Wilson approached the visitor who stood in the hall of the Wilsons' home on Beatrice Road, having been left there by the maid. Scarlet had rung the bell-pull and asked to speak to Mrs. Wilson, meaning Margaret, the mother, and had been led into the hall. But it was Catherine, the older daughter, who had come instead. Had the maid heard him to say "Miss," instead of "Mrs."?

Apparently not, as Miss Wilson added quickly: "I'm afraid my mother can't speak with you at the moment. We're at something of sixes and sevens this morning."

She was taller than her younger sister, only a couple of inches shorter than Scarlet, and slimmer of figure than Elizabeth Wilson. Her complexion was rose-colored, complementing the thick, wavy auburn hair which flowed past her slender shoulders. She had large blue eyes beneath finely-shaped eyebrows that slanted upward, giving her a slightly quizzical look. Her nose was straight and longer than it needed to be, her mouth a little too wide. Those two features, Scarlet decided, only made her beauty more individual and evident. She was looking at him steadily now, displaying an air of frankness and competence.

He thought he understood immediately why the house was at

"sixes and sevens," and the matriarch indisposed to speak to a member of the Metropolitan Police. He wasn't about to reveal his level of knowledge by mentioning their stakeout of the Reed house, however—including Elizabeth Wilson's visit there the previous day.

"I'm sorry to hear that, Miss Wilson. Is there anything I can do?"

"Thank you, but I'm afraid not. Mr. Reed, my sister's ex-fiancé, has taken ill. My sister is terribly upset, and it's a strain on our family."

Scarlet nodded. "I beg your pardon," he said. 'But what is the nature of his illness? You see, as I mentioned to your mother, I was hoping to speak with him about the fact that his name has cropped up in one of our inquiries." Members of the force had never possessed any scruples about lying to people they were interviewing, of course, though as lies went, this one was innocent enough. Yesterday, after all, he *had been* hoping to speak to Reed. There was no reason to reveal to Miss Wilson that he had done so in the meantime.

"We honestly don't know. We thought he was simply exhausted, as he's been under some strain. But three days ago, Dr. Milkwater told us it's now brain fever. And then poor Ambrose became worse overnight last night."

"What kind of strain?"

"Must I answer that?" said Catherine, her mouth firmly set.

He said, in a milder voice this time: "I apologize, Miss Wilson. I didn't mean it to sound like an interrogation. I'm simply interested in what Mr. Reed has been going through." He was well aware that he hadn't been asked into the drawing room to sit down while they talked. Presumably, the woman wanted their conversation to be brief and for him to leave.

"If you must know, Mr. Scarlet, Ambrose has been spreading himself a bit thin lately. He continues to see my sister, though he's also frequently seen around town with another woman, someone older than himself. I'm afraid he's been burning the candle at both ends and exhausted himself. But that's changing my metaphors, isn't it?"

Apparently, this Miss Wilson had more of an edge than her sister, and a tongue sharp enough to express it. Scarlet decided he liked her the more for it. He thought it was probably the reason she was speaking to him at all. She was sure to be angry at her sister's unhappy state, and placed the blame where she thought it belonged: squarely on Ambrose Reed's shoulders.

But it was the last thing she had said that interested him the most. He picked up on it immediately.

"I see. What is the name of . . . forgive me, the other woman?"

"Mrs. Bain," replied Catherine Wilson, with obvious distaste. "Mrs. Morana Bain."

Scarlet nodded.

"And can you tell me anything about this Mrs. Bain?"

Her eyes widened for a brief second, and he thought he saw a slight upturn at the corners of her mouth. Then she said, surprising him: "I'm afraid I'm being dreadfully rude, Dr. Scarlet. Would you like to continue our discussion in the drawing room?"

The small room was tastefully furnished, with morning light flooding the space from ample windows. It was too blue for his taste; but he was glad he'd made it into the inner chamber, as it were. There was something pleasant and challenging about talking to Miss Catherine Wilson, and he welcomed the opportunity to keep doing so. She spoke again as soon as they were seated: he on the couch, she in an armchair. A blue armchair.

"I believe I have the right to ask what your investigation is about, Dr. Scarlet."

"Indeed. Why?"

"Because, apparently, it involves my family." She put her hand up to halt his reply. "Yes, I understand that you have been asking about Mr. Reed. But as you can appreciate, anything affecting Ambrose has a direct influence on my sister's happiness. I realize the police need to keep their investigations undisclosed to the public. But I really don't know how I can help you if you insist on keeping us in the dark."

Well, that was plain enough. She went on before he could fashion a reply.

"Do you like guessing games, Doctor? If I guess correctly what you're really investigating, will you tell me if I've hit the mark?"

Scarlet hesitated, but not for long. He made a gesture with his right hand, palm up. *Your move.*

"You're investigating the missing children."

When he didn't answer immediately, she knew she's struck home.

She went on simply, without any triumph in her voice: "You mentioned that Ambrose's name came up in one of your inquiries. I can't imagine why, and I don't see any possible connection. Perhaps you do."

Scarlet decided there was no reason to dance around the truth. Not with this woman.

"We conducted a séance," he said, letting the flat statement sit on its own for a moment.

She didn't flinch, didn't laugh or scoff. That was very good.

"Are you talking about the reading my mother has been insisting on, to see if Mr. Reed's deceased wife has been trying to destroy the engagement?"

"Do you believe that's possible?"

"I don't believe my thoughts are important here," was her response. "Is that the séance you're talking about? I wasn't aware that it had happened."

"No, not that one," admitted Scarlet. "Another one. It's . . . a form of investigation we use if there are any clues leading in that direction." He realized how weak his explanation sounded when stated blandly like this, without any details of the situation. "Or frankly, when we don't know how else to proceed."

Her eyes were bright now, and she was leaning forward in the chair. She seemed as serious about the topic as he was.

"Can you tell me what you discovered?" she asked.

It wasn't as if he didn't want to describe to her what had taken place. He just wasn't sure how to do so. "I don't know that we discovered anything," he began. "It became strange. There was my friend—who is a medium—and two of the children's relatives. We all saw what I imagine were the same hallucinations. And at the end, someone yelled "Ambrose!" twice."

Catherine Wilson put her hand to her mouth. "Oh, my goodness. *Our* Ambrose?"

"Well, you see, that's what we don't know. But why would that particular name come up when we were asking about the missing children—especially since your mother was planning a séance about Ambrose and your sister's engagement?" He wouldn't mention that they learned from the session that the children were on the Other Side—he drew the line at that.

Her own question wasn't one he was expecting.

"Dr. Scarlet, why hasn't anyone else from the police been here? If they think that Ambrose is somehow connected—"

He interrupted her. "I'm afraid the Yard isn't generally as liberal in their thinking as you're implying," he said, with a slight smile. "To be frank, Miss Wilson, my superiors aren't aware that I conducted the séance. It's the way my friend and I have to operate sometimes."

She considered what he'd said. Then she asked, boldly, he thought: "Do you think, sir, that there is a link between your séance and Mr. Reed's sudden illness?"

"I'm afraid I'm at a loss to answer that," he replied. "At the moment, I'm trying to find out anything I can about your sister's ex-fiancé and his possible role in this matter. You mentioned a woman, a Mrs. Bain, that has come between Mr. Reed and your sister, if I may put it that way. Would it be correct to say that?"

"Yes, that is the situation."

"What can you tell me about her?" He heard a soft chime in the hall but ignored it, intent upon his question.

"Nothing, I'm afraid. She's quite an enigma to our family. As you can imagine, Ambrose hasn't volunteered any information to us about her," she added, her placid tone only underlining the angry sentiment. "I believe the general impression about town is that she isn't from around here. She has a house near Battersea Park and appears to be of independent means. Other than that, we know nothing, apart from Ambrose's apparent infatuation with her."

There was a movement of someone in the hall passing the doorway. Scarlet, seated on the couch with the door to his right, caught nothing but a glimpse of a white apron. But Catherine Wilson was sitting in the armchair facing the hall, and she saw the movement before he did, and surely who it was. She said "Excuse me," and went into the hallway. A moment later, she came back into the drawing room, holding an envelope.

"Would you pardon me for a moment, Dr. Scarlet? A letter has arrived for my sister. She is upstairs and not feeling well. The maid knew enough to hold it for me, and didn't realize I was in the drawing room. I must take it to Elizabeth."

Scarlet stood. "I understand completely," he said. "I'll leave now."

"Oh, please stay until I come down again. I'll try not to be too long."

"Of course, if you like." He remained standing until she left the room.

No more than two minutes went by before he heard sounds from upstairs. A woman was crying out and sobbing. Ten minutes later, Catherine Wilson appeared in the doorway. Her eyes were red, but somehow he knew it hadn't been her he had heard.

"I'm terribly sorry," she said, quietly. "I must tend to my sister."

He rose again, ready to leave.

"Has something happened?"

"The letter is from Mr. Reed," she replied, in the same quiet voice. "He has written that he doesn't want to see Elizabeth again." Her eyes were filling up. "He has broken it off completely, you see."

He wanted to cross to her. But he couldn't, of course.

"Dr. Scarlet?" she said, straightening to her full height, her voice stronger now.

"Yes, Miss Wilson?"

"Something is not right," she said.

CHAPTER 19

The Wind Changes

ne week. That was the thought that was uppermost in Scarlet's mind as he left the Wilsons' house a moment later. The new moon would arrive on the 16th, and stay that way for two nights. As of now, he had hardly more to go on than he had four days ago, the night of the séance.

It was almost noon, and a stiff wind had arisen from the east, hitting him as he walked down the front steps of Nine Columns. It was still early, then; at least he had the rest of the day to proceed with the investigation. He walked to the edge of the sidewalk to hail a cab. His thoughts seemed as unfocused and blown about as the gray, windy day. He realized he was still following up on the thinnest of leads, this time dealing with the Mystery Woman who had visited Reed's house yesterday evening, and perhaps on Friday as well.

Yet, her identity was surely no longer a mystery. She had to be Mrs. Bain, the woman responsible for the breaking off of Elizabeth Wilson and Ambrose Reed's engagement. It seemed curious that an older woman could so quickly have established a hold on the young man.

Normally, he wouldn't have cared one way or the other about such a private domestic matter. But the broken engagement was certainly creating a great deal of unhappiness at the Wilson residence, not only for Elizabeth, but for her capable and apparently warm-hearted sister, Catherine. Still, that was no reason for him to be concerned with the situation there.

There was one exception to that line of reasoning, and his name was Ambrose Reed. For Scarlet was now convinced that the man had something to do with the missing and murdered children. The vision that Scarlet had experienced in Reed's bedroom upon touching the deceased wife's photograph was undeniable proof—at least in his mind—that there was a connection.

The vision had been as strong as any he'd ever experienced. And if anything, his response had been even stronger: an overwhelming feeling of *possession*; the sense of a struggle between a benevolent force and an evil one; and the sudden image of the dead children, which had nevertheless disappeared so suddenly. There was no ambivalence here for him. Either Ambrose Reed or his departed wife—or both—must be involved somehow in the horror of the murdered children.

And why was Reed suddenly so incapacitated, with no discernible signs of illness that he as a physician could see? One thing was certain. He needed more information on the one person who seemed to move freely between the Reed home and the outside world: Mrs. Morana Bain.

One week.

It was time to bring in Horace Bilby.

In Scarlet's mind, Mr. Horace Bilby seemed to be as relentless as fate.

He had observed and learned things about the little man that were anything but obvious . . . until you'd spent some time in that observation. Anyone being looked at carefully by Bilby was in danger of having his or her life's secrets revealed. Bilby could sniff around old documents and ferret out information—Scarlet couldn't help thinking—that might make a dynasty fall. A target of his investigations could shoo the tiny man away (as many did), and he would simply go back to his relentless activities. He invariably found buried treasures that the rest of the world didn't know existed.

Horace Bilby was a researcher, and that was what made him dangerous.

He might be fifty or seventy, or perhaps even older. How could one tell? He appeared to be one of those people who have settled into middle age (at least!) from the time they are young.

Little Mr. Bilby also had a face which made you think you could read him like a book. You couldn't, though. He certainly looked like someone who *read* books—many, many books—and that much was true. His brow was marked by deep lines both horizontal and vertical, testifying to years of concentrated reading and scrutinizing. His face had settled into an uneven gaze, for his right eye was keen and focused, while his left drooped a bit as if it was weary of the whole affair.

His head was fringed with soft white hair—making one think of a rabbit—worn long and uncombed. His dress was, admittedly, behind the times. He always wore a neck cloth of the finest white linen wrapped around his throat above a coat of rusty black, both at least twenty years out of date. All in all, he gave the impression of a character in a Dickens novel, stranded in the here and now, perhaps, when a reader had closed the book without warning and he couldn't get back inside.

Bilby didn't care about his appearance, or anything else for that matter that anyone could determine. He had a single mania, which was why he was meeting now with William Scarlet and Django Pierce-Jones at the former's house in Chelsea.

Mr. Bilby lived to read. As a young man, he had labored at a position that required much looking over of accounts and ledgers; had gone on to oversee catalogs and archives; and had finally established his own private concern offering discreet and in-depth research of existing records of any and all kinds. So discreet, in fact, that the firm had no name. Destiny had missed a beat by not giving him the last name of Wordsworth, which would have looked capital on the office door of a research firm. Alas, he was Bilby, and he had opted for no name on that door.

To Scarlet and Pierce-Jones, however, he was simply The Reader.

"We would like you to look into a woman named Mrs. Morana Bain," Scarlet informed him now in the comfortable drawing room of One, Beaufort Circle. "She is a lady of some forty years or so, and apparently of independent means. She currently lives in London, in Lurline Gardens near Battersea Park. We don't know if she has other houses elsewhere. Nothing is known of her background, as far as we have been able to learn. She speaks with a slight accent: country and language unknown. We would like you to find out everything you can about her."

He waited for the little man to catch up in his notes.

"Ah, yes. Ah, yes," said Bilby. His voice was always not much more than a whisper, and Scarlet and Pierce-Jones had gotten used to leaning in slightly and perking up their ears whenever The Reader spoke.

"The usual sources, I imagine," Bilby whispered on, mostly to himself. "Newspapers, society publications, notices of events during last Season and previous ones." His hand caressed his chin now: "Delivery records to the house, current and former employees." A more open expression blossomed on his face: "Whatever banking records I might be able to look at, police reports, legal cases, property records. . . . Ah!" Wide open expression now: "Restaurant and theater staff . . . they may have something to contribute. And dressmakers—mustn't forget dressmakers!"

He looked up at them after this litany and asked: "Any unusual sources you're aware of that I might consider, gentlemen?" To Scarlet, the man's mumbled list already seemed exhaustive, and he answered in the negative.

"Fine! Fine!" said Bilby, nodding his head vigorously. He

suddenly had the unmistakable appearance of a dog who has just picked up a scent.

"And your fee?" Django asked.

"Oh, I'll send you a bill, certainly I will."

More nodding . . . or was it sniffing?

"It all depends on the work I and my staff do. And the results, of course." He went back to musing to himself about sources of information, excluding the other two men from his attention entirely.

The grubby details of commerce had never interested Mr. Bilby.

At 4.30 that afternoon, a messenger arrived at the front door of the house with a letter addressed to Scarlet. It was from Dr. Milkwater, and dated that day. It was brief and succinct. That physician regretted having to withdraw forthwith from the care of Mr. Ambrose Reed of 65, Bayswater Road, London. Scarlet had been recommended as his replacement. Would Mr. Scarlet be so kind as to reply by return message as to whether he could take on the case? If so, could he possibly visit the patient this evening and take up his care?

That was all. Nothing about Milkwater's reason for having to withdraw from Reed's case. And nothing, for that matter, concerning who had recommended him, Scarlet, for the job.

This certainly put him in a delicate position. If Reed were officially the target of a criminal investigation—or even a party involved in an investigation—it would be a clear conflict of interest for Scarlet to be administering the man's care. But Reed wasn't officially a party in any investigation by the Yard. Scarlet was deliberately keeping the stakeout of Reed's home from Mallinson; and he had no intention of letting his superior learn about it.

Also, if Mallinson did find out about Scarlet administering to Reed, his displeasure would probably be slight—he was a physician and fellow surgeon, after all. What *would* set Mallinson off would be learning that Scarlet had carried out a private surveillance of Reed, without letting the Yard know. Scarlet thought he was past worrying about it, however. The truth was, he couldn't pass up the opportunity to get close to Reed and find out what his involvement was in the murders. And he couldn't divulge to his superior that he'd discovered this avenue of investigation through his psychic ability . . . with a séance added for good measure.

He would keep his silence and proceed with his line of inquiry. In for a penny, in for a pound.

He wrote a brief note for the messenger to return to Milkwater. He expressed his regret that the doctor found it necessary to resign from the case; he would be only too happy to step in, etc., etc. Not for the first time, he gave thanks to his part-time status as an assistant chief surgeon with the Metropolitan Police, which left time for a private practice.

And sometimes, a private investigation.

Ambrose Reed looked much worse than he had just three days earlier, thought Scarlet as he took the man's pulse that evening. The flushed look was gone, and his skin was no longer hot to the touch. Not an infection, then. And the brain fever seemed to have subsided. On the other hand, he looked more drawn and tired, an appearance accentuated by a few days' stubble. And he'd lost weight. His features were as handsome as ever, but somehow his face looked smaller. Was it possible for a man to actually *shrink* as a result of an illness?

Scarlet put such poppycock out of his mind as he concentrated on a diagnosis. Exhaustion, that old standby, came to mind. He was sufficiently forward-looking in his profession to realize that a diagnosis might only be a clue to what was underlying a condition, i.e., the thing which needed to be treated. He was always amazed at how many of his colleagues didn't think this way, considering, say, a fever as the illness to be treated, not the infection or mental trauma that caused it in the first place.

What was it that was sending Ambrose Reed into a debilitative state and draining his energy and stamina? Scarlet's physician and surgeon's mind took over and he studied the physical signs closely. Like every case, there was something here he could learn from to benefit his patients in his surgery and as a house physician at St George's Hospital.

He was struck by the expression in Reed's eyes, which seemed an odd combination of exhilaration and sadness. And something else . . . was it fear? For a moment he wished that his father, James Scarlet, were still alive so he could consult with him on the case. As a psychiatric doctor, the elder Dr. Scarlet might see something in Reed's condition that he would be able to diagnose more readily than his son could.

The patient's sharpness of mind and tongue hadn't changed, however. Scarlet found that out quickly enough.

"So, I've been handed off to you, it seems," Reed said as his pulse was being taken. "Was Dr. Milkwater stumped? Do I have an exotic disease he hasn't seen before, and that has made him run in the other direction? . . . Milkwater. What a perfectly dreadful name! How could you succeed at anything if that's your name?"

Scarlet's smile was measured and meaningless: the smile all doctors use at moments like this. "No, nothing fancy in the way of a diagnosis, I'm afraid, so you won't become famous for it. Your paintings will have to take on that duty. From what I can see, it's simple exhaustion."

"Well, that part is bloody well right. I *am* exhausted." He made a dismissive sound. "Now that you've brought it up, I've been advised against painting. Do you concur, as you doctors say?"

"I'd say it all depends—"

"Never mind," Reed said, closing his eyes and sinking back on the pillow.

"Rest now, and I'll check in on you tomorrow," said Scarlet, rising and gathering his things. But he halted halfway to the door. "By the way," he said, "I'm a bit surprised that Dr. Milkwater recommended me as his replacement. I was under the impression he didn't like me."

"Oh, it wasn't him," Reed replied, his eyes still closed. "It was a friend of mine, Mrs. Bain. . . . Good night, Mr. Scarlet."

"Good night," said the other, confused.

On his way out, he glanced at the framed photograph of Reed's first wife, Mrs. Mary Reed, where it sat in the same spot on the mantlepiece. The photo had changed. The woman's tight black curls, the dress she wore, the part of her bosom that showed above the dress's square neckline—all of these were all the same. But the face was that of a skeleton. Next to the picture frame, a silver pitcher rested on top of two books which were laid flat on the mantle, just as it had three days earlier. When Scarlet had entered the room a few minutes ago, the pitcher had been filled with fresh pink-tinged hydrangeas of the season. Now, the flowers were desiccated and dead.

CHAPTER 20

Thomas Geach, Private Inquiry Agent

hat same evening, Catherine Wilson sat across from a greasy and loathsome-looking man in the drawing room of her home, Nine Columns. The man was sitting on the couch, in the exact spot where a much more attractive man, Dr. Scarlet, had sat just that morning. She wasn't expecting this visit so quickly, as she had only sent a telegram to the man's office earlier that day. But who knew what kind of schedule a person like this kept?

His calling card read: *Thomas Geach, Private Inquiry Agent.* Apparently, then, she had the right man. Sitting in the same wing chair she had occupied that morning, Catherine held the card in her hand, as if, like a chess piece, she wasn't committed to making this move until she let go of it.

She sighed inwardly, thinking that this person was nothing more or less than what one should expect when hiring a private investigator.

She decided that Mr. Geach looked like a snake with dark glasses on. Yes, it was evening already and she couldn't imagine how he made his way through the streets with his vision obstructed in that way. Perhaps the glasses were a necessary part of a private detective's uniform, to keep them from being recognized. She doubted it, however. It seemed merely an affectation.

The man wasn't small, but—was it the inscrutability of the

expression behind the glasses?—seemed somehow as though he would slip through your fingers if you tried to pin him down. His suit was black, but oddly set off by a crimson waistcoat and ruffled neckpiece of the same color. He wore a black hat of the type Caroline believed was called a John Bull Topper, a silk top hat with a shortened crown. His mouth was set in a downturned expression, while his eyebrows seemed to be permanently in the act of asking a question. Both, she supposed, were necessary characteristics in the private inquiries game. Mr. Geach sat on the couch with his right hand resting on a silver-topped cane, which no doubt had a sword hidden inside it.

"Her name is Morana Bain," Caroline said, continuing their conversation. When the man continued to stare at her, she added: "Don't you want to take notes or something?"

"No need, Madam." The voice, at least, was human enough, and his tongue didn't dart out. Thank heaven for small favors, thought Caroline.

"You understand that I want observations only—where she goes, who she meets with, and things like that. You mustn't engage her directly."

"I know my business, if you don't mind me sayin' so. I imagine you want to know if she's steppin' out with someone, if you know what I mean. Usually, it's the fella you have in mind I follow, but it'll work this way too."

Though the exact opposite was true, she didn't want to tell him that. Or anything, for that matter, other than what was absolute necessary.

"And you're to report only to me."

"I'm the soul of discretion, I am, Madam," replied Geach, sounding slightly offended.

"You may telegram me when you're ready to report. Please don't come here to the house. Here are funds to cover your expenses." She handed him an envelope. "Let me know if you need more."

Geach touched the sturdy rim of his hat, then pulled at the end of his nose. "Ta, m'um. Anything else, then?"

"That will be all. Thank you, Mr. Geach."

"I'll be off, then," he said unnecessarily, standing.

Caroline, not wanting to involve the house staff in any of this, saw him out. Then she stood by the window, watching him walk off into the night.

"Now we'll see what we can find out about you, Morana Bain," she said aloud.

From her tone, the actual words might have been: "Hurt my dear sister, will you?"

CHAPTER 21

Three Mysteries

At the start of the next day in his surgery, Scarlet felt that he was nearly useless to his patients. He couldn't seem to keep his thoughts on track. A woman had to explain to him twice that it was her husband's symptoms she was explaining to him, not her own (the man simply refused to come in himself, and had done so for years). After a boy's mother explained how he had injured his right arm ("Is it broken, Mr. Scarlet?"), Scarlet had begun to examine the boy's left arm. And so, the morning went.

He was quite sure now that Mary Reed's photograph hadn't actually been changed when he'd looked at it, last night in Reed's bedroom. He knew that, had anyone else looked at the photo, they would have seen Mary's small dark features, not a woman's form with a skeleton's face. And he was sure the flowers in the pitcher on the mantle were as healthy as they had been when he entered the room, not withered and dead as he saw them when he left. It was simply one of his visions.

But why had it taken place? He hadn't touched anything or made physical contact with Reed in the bed. It was true that sometimes a place he visited elicited a vision as he stood in it. But that was rare. And the stimuli didn't change: if touching someone or something or standing in a location brought on a vision-state, it stayed that way as long as he remained in that place. The link of immediate stimulus and response didn't change, a fact his medical mind accepted without question. Yet he'd been in Reed's bedroom previously—in fact, he'd been there for some time last night before he saw the altered photograph and flowers.

Why were things happening differently this time? It was a mystery.

He was better focused when dealing with that morning's third, fourth, and fifth patients. The sixth, however, set things off in an entirely new direction.

This was a teamster, brought in by the manager of a mercantile warehouse. The man had been the driver of a wagon load of merchandise delivered that morning to the building. A barrel had begun to roll off the back of the wagon, splintering a large wooden plank at the side of the wagon's bed, and the teamster, rushing forward to halt the barrel's movement, had stepped straight into the sharp point of the now-splintered wood. The point had penetrated his arm, lifting up a three-inch-long section of skin and muscle.

The warehouse manager had had the foresight to break off a piece of the plank, leaving it in the arm rather than pulling it out and causing further bleeding. The manager's actions, and the fact that the wound was an avulsion—a tearing wound rather than an incision, where multiple blood vessels might have been sliced through—meant that the accident was much less serious than it might have been. The man was in serious pain, of course, and his arm and sleeve were bloodied. But the wood shard had missed the superficial radial artery, so the bleeding was relatively limited.

It *was* a bloody wound, nevertheless. Because the man was young and strong and wasn't complaining of the pain he was undoubtedly feeling, Scarlet limited the laudanum he administered to ten drops, given in brandy. Then he got to work, with his assistant Archibald Hunt washing the area while he used pressure, a repositioning of the muscles back to their normal positions, and sutures to repair what was essentially a dramatic-appearing but minor wound.

He found himself struggling through the actual work, however. When he removed the shard and lifted the section of avulsed tissue, for some reason the sight of the small field of blood seemed to penetrate his brain, and he was abruptly in a vision.

He was in the operating theatre at St George's Hospital, and everywhere—on the floor, and on the walls, on his clothes—were splashes and pools of blood. *Rivers* of blood.

I am so deep in blood, he thought.

He realized that it was his nightmare of a few months ago: of the young-but-suddenly-older woman on the operating table. Anne Pusey, her name was. And her father, there for some reason as well. She'd died on the table but had become animated again, and there was a nightmarish wedding ceremony where he was getting married to her.

What had she said to him at the end of the ceremony?

"My enemy."

He saw it all again now, but kept working. At last, while he was suturing the man's arm, the scenes from the nightmare faded from his vision.

Why had this dead-yet-alive-again girl said, 'My enemy?' And what was the connection with blood—why had the sight of it thrown him back into that dream?

It was another mystery.

He visited Reed that afternoon, expecting to find evidence of further physical decline. But that wasn't the case. For one thing, Reed was up and about. Scarlet found him in the hall, dressed in a scarlet robe and with a cup and saucer in his hand, about to walk up the stairs to his bedroom on the second floor.

"I insisted on fetching the tea myself, Doctor," he explained, as though to keep the nurse out of trouble.

"I see. You're feeling better, then."

"Oh, yes. I *did* get out of bed, you see." Then he turned and, with what Scarlet thought was almost a floating movement, began walking up the stairs. No, not floating. More like automatic motions—muscular actions somehow not dependent upon the mind.

Scarlet followed the strangely moving Reed up the stairs to the bedroom, where his gaze went immediately to Mary Reed's photograph and the silver pitcher on the mantlepiece. Both were entirely normal, including the still-fresh hydrangeas in the vase. When he looked back, Reed was sitting on the bed, balancing the tea cup and saucer on his lap, his legs dangling near but not on the floor. He had a curious expression on his face as he looked at the other man, like that of a precocious child. Scarlet had the irrational thought that Reed had seen him looking at the photograph and pitcher, knowing the reason why his visitor's gaze had gone there.

"Would you have any objection to my going to my studio to work?" Reed asked suddenly.

"I don't think that's wise," Scarlet answered. "Let's see how you're doing." And he opened his bag, not recognizing that he was displaying the medical professional's typical disregard for a patient's concerns.

Reed's vital signs were normal, and he was definitely past his earlier fevered condition. He looked thinner and more drawn than he had yesterday, however. On the other hand, his eyes were brighter, as if all his energy now resided there. Scarlet also didn't like the man's color. His face was waxy, and looked as if it would feel that way to the touch. And his gestures continued to look automatic, in the fashion Scarlet had noticed a moment ago, as though his movements lacked any intentions. It was certainly very odd, and Scarlet couldn't think of any medical reason behind it.

A third mystery, then.

Could it be that the almost burning look in Reed's eyes and his purposeless movements were simply the result of him feeling caged—the artist kept away from his work too long? The truth was, there wasn't anything medically evident that could be used to justify keeping the man in his bedroom. Perhaps getting back to his work was the best thing for him, after all.

There was another consideration in Scarlet's mind as well. He had nothing in the way of evidence to prove that Reed was involved with the children's disappearance—only his vision when he touched the photograph, and his sense of two entities warring with each other. And the children's faces he saw. It wasn't enough to point him in any definite direction. Of course, Bilby was on the trail of the other possible lead: Mrs. Bain. If there were anything to be found, The Reader would uncover it.

That was what Scarlet was expecting . . . with six days until the new moon.

"I think it would be all right for you to go to your studio," he said at the end of the examination, giving in to his patient. "But pace yourself, Mr. Reed. You've just been through an illness, and you don't have your full strength yet. And would you kindly give me the address of your studio so I have it handy?"

Reed smiled, the precocious child who, once again, gets his way.

"I would be delighted, Doctor."

They could just as easily watch Reed's movements at his studio than at his house, Scarlet told himself as he walked down the stairs to the front foyer. More easily, actually. There were just too many intrigues going on in any good-sized house in this Age of Queen Victoria.

CHAPTER 22

An Unusual Circumstance

Late in the afternoon of Wednesday 12 October—or three days after Catherine Wilson had engaged the services of Thomas Geach, Private Inquiry Agent—she received a telegram from him delivered to her home. The handwritten message on the yellow Post Office Telegraphs form read:

> Nothing firm. Following up on unusual circumstance, however. Will be in touch when no more.
>
> Geach

Reading the last sentence again, she thought that Mr. Geach was certainly poorly educated. Or perhaps he had been in a hurry when he wrote it.
She certainly hoped it wasn't an omen.
Then again, given all this talk about séances, how could one be sure?

CHAPTER 23

Thursday – Friday, 13 - 14 October

The news from Horace Bilby was stunning, even startling. Scarlet received the longish letter from The Reader at home early Thursday evening. He had known that Bilby didn't trust any technology as advanced as the telegraph, and that he would certainly be in contact via a handwritten note. He was also expecting that whatever he received from his investigator would include a *précis* of the research he and his staff had done to date.

Quickly scanning the list of sources and resources Bilby had consulted—each entry written out beautifully in Bilby's elegant hand—he skipped to the conclusion:

> We are, unfortunately, unable to compile satisfactory material on the subject. To say that Mrs. Morana Bain has left a dearth of information on herself and her history would be an inadequate statement in itself. I have seldom—nay, never—run across a similar situation. Our inability to deliver any results whatsoever is complete and inexplicable.
>
> In view of our absolute failure to satisfy you in the task you have entrusted to my firm, I must, of course, abjure any payment whatsoever.

Please accept my sincere apologies for our disappointing performance in this assignment.

Your faithful servant, Sir,
Horace W. Bilby

Scarlet was disappointed, of course. But he was more amazed. Despite The Reader's old-world manners, he headed the best private research organization in England where documentation was concerned. For him to come up empty in this way was unfathomable.

What could it mean?

He had a whisky and soda as he pondered the question, then another. When the clock struck midnight he decided he would turn in.

It was now Friday, the 14th of October.

CHAPTER 24

Autopsy

wo hours later, Scarlet found himself pounding on the doors of Hell. He had to get inside to gather evidence he knew was in there. Then the noise became someone's fist hammering on the front door of his house; and that woke Scarlet, his man Jeffries, and the cook and housekeeper Mrs. Bennie all at the same moment. The servants' rooms were on the third floor and Scarlet's bedroom was on the second, so he was the first to reach the door and whatever form of chaos it was that wanted to enter his house.

Filling up the frame once the door was opened was a very large and stalwart policeman Scarlet recognized by sight but not by name. The uniformed constable looked steady and unexcited, as if beating doors down with his fist was all in a night's work—or in this case, an early morning's work.

Hannity, that was his name. Sergeant Hannity . . . Big Jim Hannity.

"I'm sorry, Mr. Scarlet," Hannity said, though he didn't look it. "There's been a murder. If possible, they'd—"

"Where and when, Sergeant?" Scarlet cut him off. Calls to leave home in the middle of the night were no novelty for a police surgeon. He'd learn who had sent for him on their way to wherever they were going.

"Soho, sir. And as near as can be determined, late last night. Body of a man discovered in an alley off Berwick Street."

Body of a man. Not a gentleman, then.

"Step in, Sergeant," Scarlet said, and when Hannity had: "Give me five minutes. Can I get you anything . . . brandy, whisky?"

"Kind of you, Mr. Scarlet. But no. I'll just wait here, if I may."

Six minutes later, after letting Jeffries know where he was going, Scarlet followed Hannity out to the cab that was waiting in the brisk night air to take them to the Yard.

The horse was now clattering its way through the wide archway of 5, Whitehall Place, Westminister. The building was across the street from the original Metropolitan Police headquarters at 4, Whitehall Place, with its eponymous entrance on Great Scotland Yard. The building they were headed for, No. 5, was one of the six new addresses the police force had expanded into over the past few years, not counting the acquisition of some stables in the same area.

The two men stepped from the cab even before it had stopped moving, then walked briskly through the courtyard to the door of No. 5. They descended the stairway leading to the lower level, where the post-mortem facilities were housed. On one level lower still, in the sub-basement, was the morgue, which was equipped with a lift to bring bodies up to the dissecting room.

As Scarlet walked toward that room now, he noticed once again the makeshift feel of this hall and the rooms on either side. He knew that his superior, Dr. Mallinson, had fought a series of heroic battles with the Police Commissioner: first, to get the basement area allocated to the medical department, and second, to provide sufficient funding for materials and supplies.

The dismal hour—the coldest part of the night—and the reason for his visit now added another layer of cheerlessness to the somber surroundings. The medical personnel of the Yard didn't joke much as they went about their usual post-mortem duties here in the basement of No. 5. They left that to the hospital morgues and autopsy rooms, which, if just as stark, were on the whole more congenial places.

They reached the doorway to the dissecting room. Sgt. Hannity stepped to the right side of the door and immediately assumed a stance—legs slightly farther apart than usual, hands behind the back—which clearly announced he was now on guard duty.

Scarlet entered and walked to the middle of the room, where a fully-clothed male cadaver lay on a dissecting table. Standing around the table and chatting with each other were Mallinson, Henry Pollock, who was another departmental assistant surgeon like himself, and two other men whom Scarlet didn't recognize. He took them for observers from the Criminal Investigation Department (CID), a special unit of the detective branch. Perhaps the deceased was an important personage. It was more likely, however, that the sensational and still unsolved series of children's disappearances had activated more departments than usual. All four men around the table were in street dress.

"Dr. Scarlet!" Mallinson called out briskly as he approached, most likely using his title for the benefit of the CID men. "Thank you for coming."

Mallinson introduced him to the two men who were, indeed, representatives of CID. Scarlet nodded, half-listening to their names and forgetting them immediately. He was focused on the body on the dissecting table.

It was a ghastly sight, even for an experienced police surgeon. All of the exposed areas outside the clothes—the head, neck, and wrists—displayed the art of butchery. Both hands were missing, removed more or less cleanly and leaving visible cross-sections at the wrists of muscle, fat, severed blood vessels, and circles of bone sawn through.

But the head was where the murder or murderers had exercised great care and devotion. For what was done here had taken time to accomplish. The eyes had been carefully removed along with the surrounding orbital tissue. The effect of this procedure was a face turned into a mask of horror. Removing only the eyeballs would have resulted in a mostly closed look to the eyes as the lids filled in the deficit. But this man's lids had been removed as well. In fact, enough tissue had been cut away so that the result was a face with two large, perfectly round black holes where the eyes should have been. It was a visage from a nightmare—something from one's worst dreams or fears.

The other deficit was just below that, where the nose should have been. All that was there now was a deep, triangular hole with ragged edges. Scarlet gazed with some amazement at how hollowed-out a face can look with both eyes and the nose gone! It was a stark reminder that the skull is the true framework of the face we show the world, made acceptable by a thin covering of skin. Skin, cartilage, arteries, veins, muscles, tendons, fasciae, and nerves . . . all of it was so close at hand, yet so easily removed.

The last piece of outward savagery they could see was at the lips. They were sewn shut, with common catgut.

"We waited to start the necropsy until you arrived, Dr. Scarlet," Mallinson was saying. "You will be assisting me. Dr. Pollock will take notes."

'Assisting' Mallinson usually meant standing by and thrilling to the great man's technique and skill. In truth, he was a brilliant anatomist and one of the best medical examiners Scarlet had ever observed in action.

"This man's name, by the way," his chief said, consulting his notes, "is Thomas Geach. Judging by the revolver we found on his person and various other instruments of the trade, he appears to have been a private investigator. We found no identification indicating he was a police officer. He still had his wallet with money in it, so robbery doesn't seem to have been the motive for his murder."

"Do we know anything about him?" Scarlet asked. "What about his movements around the time of his death? Were there any witnesses?"

"I'm afraid not," replied Mallinson.

Scarlet directed his next question to the group at large. "Anything from the scene?"

One of the CID men answered. "Nothing left behind that could be found last night. We'll know better at first light, of course."

"How much blood was there in the alley where he was found?" Scarlet asked him.

"Very little."

"So, the murder was committed elsewhere."

"Not necessarily," said Mallinson. "There was sufficient blood present on the stones that we think at least some of the disfiguration took place there. But not nearly enough to account for all of *this*," he concluded, indicating the body.

"That's strange," Scarlet observed. "It isn't likely that someone would do some of this in one location, move the body, then get back to work."

No one had any answer to that.

Mallinson had taken off his coat and was now unbuttoning his waistcoat. When no one else moved, he said: "Gentlemen?"

It was time to begin.

The cadaver was stripped and a rectal thermometer inserted to determine the degree of algor mortis, or cooling of the body after death. The reading was 91.9 degrees Fahrenheit. Allowing for the standard interval of temperature plateau which lasted 1-3 hours before a body began to cool (the three physicians decided to use 1.5 hours as their estimate), that gave a time of death of around 10.00 p.m. the previous night. They reasoned that that was probably close to the mark, because of three factors: (1) The victim hadn't been left in the open air fully or even partially unclothed; (2) Judging from the state of the body when found and the state of his clothing, he most likely hadn't exerted himself greatly before death; and (3) He obviously didn't have a female's greater proportion of subcutaneous fat. The first of these three facts would have accelerated the cadaver's loss of temperature, while the last two would have retarded it.

Hence, the time of death was probably accurate based on algor mortis.

Also, the body was discovered in the alley a little before 11.00 p.m. So, again, the time of death matched.

Finally, rigor mortis or stiffening of the muscles was present only in the lower jaw, face, and neck. Since rigor is first observed two to six hours after death, and begins in exactly those locations on the body that were indicated here, the time of death of approximately 10.00 p.m. the previous evening held firm.

A head block was now placed under the shoulders to raise the chest area for easier incision. Dr. Mallinson was standing to the right of and level with the head, while Dr. Pollock had placed himself to the left of the table and a few steps back to take notes and be out of the way. Scarlet was positioned on Mallinson's right, at the cadaver's waist. There, he would be able to observe the dissection while not interfering with Mallinson's right hand. The chief surgeon began his narrative. As always, his voice became steady and even more emotionless than usual—a voice that was entirely clinical in nature.

"This is Dr. Edward Mallinson. The time is 4.20 a.m. on 14 October 1887. Dissection of a cadaver identified as Thomas Geach, approximately six hours after death. The body is that of a strongly built and well-nourished man approximately in his mid-thirties. Height is five feet, nine and a half inches. Hair brown. Beginning the external examination. . ."

In any autopsy, prior to the familiar Y-shaped incision and the interior examination, the body is examined externally for any fresh or healed wounds, bruises, or scars, and any identifying marks. The dissector will sometimes look slowly and carefully over the entire surface of the body at a distance of only inches, and Mallinson did that now.

Aside from the horrific injuries to the face and the amputation of both hands, there were no visible external wounds, with one exception. An approximately 3" longitudinal or vertical incision was visible in the upper left thigh near the groin. Apart from the obvious fact that it had been done with a very sharp instrument (a scalpel?), they could tell nothing else until they went inside.

The body lying before them necessitated an additional step before that one, however. Dr. Mallinson carefully removed the sutures from the lips, and explored the oral cavity. He immediately discovered that the deceased had also undergone a glossectomy, or surgical removal of the entire tongue.

A moment later, he said to Scarlet:

"Hand me the otoscope and ear speculum, will you?" He peered into both ears with the device; then for the benefit of Dr. Pollock who was taking notes, said: "Both eardrums have been perforated, apparently by a dull, pointed instrument."

Mallinson now went in. The Y-incision was made from each shoulder, running down at an angle to the sternum, where it then continued downward to the pubic area. The skin was retracted and shears were used to open the chest cavity and remove the sternum and the rib cage.

The litany began as Dr. Mallinson sliced and peeled through the body's layers to lift, examine, and weigh organs before removing them to get to organs deeper within.

"Lungs are of normal appearance. Right lung weighs two pounds four ounces, left lung, two pounds.

"Pericardium is healthy.

"Heart, nine ounces. The left ventricle is contracted. The thoracic aorta is collapsed.

"The surface of the liver is smooth and reddish-brown in appearance and is soft. No abnormalities noted. Four pounds, fourteen ounces.

"Spleen, six ounces and soft.

"Kidneys, ten ounces each.

"Bladder is distended with urine. Healthy-looking.

"Pancreas healthy.

And when it was time to examine the deep cut present in the upper left thigh:

"A longitudinal incision is visible on the left leg approximately two inches to the left of the pubic symphysis, and about two and one-half inches below the inguinal ligament. The cut proceeds downward for . . . let's see, three and one-eighths inches from the superior portion of the femoral head. Well, this is interesting. The incision longitudinally separates the deep fascia but stops before penetrating the femoral vessel itself."

He bent forward to peer more deeply at the wound, and the two other physicians sympathetically did the same. Mallinson's voice continued as he looked at the wound from close-up, shifting the position of his head to see it from different angles.

"The femoral artery appears to have a fine round hole perforating its surface, approximately, oh, three-sixteenths of an inch in diameter. The edges of this perforation are clean and well-defined."

By this point, all three doctors knew the cause of death. Proper necropsy procedures required, however, that the rest of the dissection should proceed until the autopsy was complete. Blood had been drawn for chemical analysis, and tissue samples taken from each organ. Dr. Mallinson proceeded now to remove the brain. An incision was made in the back of the skull, and the scalp was sliced and pulled forward to reveal the skull itself. The cranium was then opened with the skull saw, and the brain lifted out of the cranial vault. Its appearance was entirely normal. None of the physicians saw the necessity of removing the spinal cord.

The time was now 5.36 a.m. Dr. Mallinson took a deep breath and stretched, his hands bracing his lower back as he arched upwards. He placed a sheet on the remains, then crossed to the sink to wash his hands. He removed his apron and placed it in a cloth bin to be laundered, then put his frock coat back on. Drs. Scarlet and Pollock met him at the head of the dissecting table.

"Your opinion as to the cause of death, gentlemen?" the chief police surgeon asked. He might have been questioning students who had just observed an autopsy in a medical school's operating theatre.

There was little question in this case, and Henry Pollock announced:

"Exsanguination."

He was undoubtedly correct. To these three men's experienced eyes, the signs were unmistakable. At first glance, that wasn't apparent. The victim appeared to have had an olive complexion, so there wasn't the obvious sign of extreme pallor one observed in a fair-skinned person who had died of blood loss.

But the appearance—and especially, the weight—of the heart and kidneys was the giveaway. When a massive loss of blood has occurred, the heart will weigh in at up to twenty-five percent less than its normal weight, and the kidneys around fifteen percent less. This man's heart weighed nine ounces, when it should have come in at twelve to fifteen ounces. Likewise, the kidneys weighed ten ounces, instead of the twelve ounces that would be normal for a man of this size and weight. The collapsed thoracic aorta in the heart was another sign that Thomas Geach had bled to death. Finally, there was the symmetrical hole in the femoral artery, an odd finding but one that was, along with the other evidence, strongly determinative of what had caused this man's death. As far as they could tell from the lack of massive bleeding around the facial and oral wounds, the disfiguration had occurred after death.

Scarlet would check in with the detectives later in the day to learn if there were any leads or other developments in the case. Otherwise, it was time to go home. He was bone-tired from little sleep, the early-morning rush to the Yard, then standing inactive during the slow procedures of autopsy. Unfortunately, getting some sleep was not possible. He had patients to see this morning in his home surgery, starting a little more than two hours from now.

Even that rest-time was apparently about to be whittled away, however, as Mallinson signaled that he wanted to talk to him privately. As Dr. Pollock looked over his notes, the two men moved away from the autopsy table.

"This is going to look like another cock-up to the public," his superior said to him. "The children's disappearance, and now this." With a start, Scarlet remembered that Mallinson didn't know anything about the séance, and that the children—if the events of the sitting had been accurate—were dead. Sgt. Jessey, who had been present at the séance but who also knew of Mallinson's deep disapproval of any occult activity on Scarlet's part, had kept his mouth shut. In addition, Jessey didn't consider the events unfolding in a séance as proof of any kind in a murder investigation, which was to Scarlet's advantage.

Still, catching himself like this was a reminder. No matter how tired he was, he could never let his guard down with his superior.

"It's going to seem like a killing ground out there," Mallinson went on. "As though any bloody maniac can take a knife and carve up people in the streets. People are already on edge because of the missing children."

He gave Scarlet a piercing look.

"Do you have any news to tell me?" he asked.

"No, sir," answered Scarlet, knowing that Mallinson was referring to the missing children's case, not the Geach murder. "The best course seems to be the one we're pursuing: increasing the manpower on the streets for the two nights of the new moon." Pierce-Jones had shared his insight on the lunar cycle with the Yard, of course, since the police had officially called him in to help with the missing children.

Suddenly, Mallinson seemed as tired as Scarlet felt.

"Christ, what day is it . . . Friday?" He looked upward at the weak light starting to show through the high windows of the basement space. "Hard to tell, with a schedule like this." He looked back at Scarlet, his belligerence apparently gone. "Patients today?"

"A few this morning," the other replied.

"Well, all right, then. Thanks for your help ton— this morning, rather."

Scarlet thought of replying: "My pleasure, sir," but decided he didn't need to come across as stupid as well as exhausted.

CHAPTER 25

A Hearse Goes By

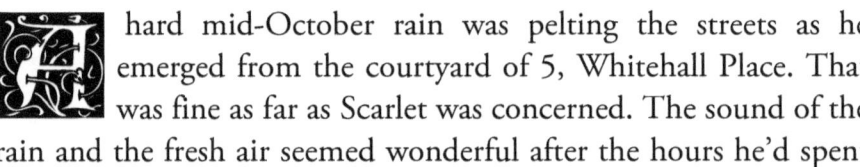hard mid-October rain was pelting the streets as he emerged from the courtyard of 5, Whitehall Place. That was fine as far as Scarlet was concerned. The sound of the rain and the fresh air seemed wonderful after the hours he'd spent in the grim place he was leaving. The rain had started sometime during his hours in the Yard's mortuary, so he had no umbrella. He expected it wouldn't be difficult to find a cab at this hour of the morning, however, before all of London spilled out of its homes, rooming houses, doss houses, and alleys.

As he reached the sidewalk, a hearse clattered by on the cobblestones of Whitehall Place directly in front of him. It seemed a fitting sight for this particular morning. Its roof was piled with flower arrangements, though the central rectangular section was empty. Since the flowers hadn't been deposited at a grave site, the driver must be on his way to collect the guest of honour.

The hearse seemed a pretty thing: shiny black with silver ornamentation and drawn by two perfectly matched Flemish black horses, the standard for a funeral carriage. Death, he reflected, had never looked so good. Of course, it never looked good, once you saw it close-up and stripped of any niceties. All one needed to do to learn that lesson was go through the door he had just come out of and down the stairs, where Death was receiving visitors without any fancy dress.

He was wrong about available cabs, and decided to walk toward Whitehall and its greater level of traffic. A newsboy at the corner was shouting about the headline in the morning edition of *The Daily Post*. That happened to be the newspaper owned by James Scorgie, one of the members of Scarlet's own Society for Supernatural and Psychic Research. Apparently Scorgie, a newspaperman to the core, hadn't wasted any time in squeezing Thomas Geach's corpse, until money fell from it. The headlines screamed:

GHASTLY MURDER IN SOHO ALLEY
MAN'S FACE BRUTALLY CARVED AWAY
Scotland Yard Hunting Monster

For once, Scarlet thought, the headlines didn't exceed the horror of the thing itself. He bought a paper and saw that, unsurprisingly, the actual story was anemic. The *Post* would have had to go to its morning deadline with the few facts that were available last night, sprinkling them over a mountain of conjecture. The paper at least had Geach's name correct, as his identity had been quickly known at the scene from his wallet. But he would learn nothing else from the rag. He tucked the paper under his arm and finally found a cab.

Fortunately, what he'd told Mallinson was the truth: he had only morning appointments today. For some reason, patients shied away from visiting doctors' surgeries on Fridays, especially Friday afternoons. Today, he was thankful for it. He looked forward to a leisurely lunch and using the rest of the day to plan his next move. Django would be stopping by for dinner. At that point, they would have exactly two days—or nights—until the new moon.

He heard the bell-pull in the middle of his last scheduled session and wondered who it could be. His assistant and secretary,

Archibald Hunt, would take care of it, of course. It must be a last-minute patient—an injury, or the sudden onset of acute symptoms which hadn't allowed for making an appointment.

But he was wrong. A moment after his last patient had left the surgery, the door opened again. Catherine Wilson stood in the doorway, looking lost. Her eyes were wide and red, and she appeared shaken. It was something of a shock to Scarlet to see this normally self-possessed and handsome woman in such a state.

"I'm sorry for coming unannounced," she declared, in a distracted way. "I didn't . . . that is . . ."

Will crossed to her. He took her arm and led her to a chair.

"Are you all right? What is it?"

She looked up at him. "He's dead. And it's my fault. I hired him and now he's dead. I don't know what to do."

He had fetched brandy and brought it to her before he spoke. Now, he gently helped her to take a sip.

"Catherine, who is dead? I don't know who you're talking about. Will you explain it to me?"

"Geach," she replied. "Thomas Geach," she said, and the words were like a whip lashing his face.

"*What?*" he exclaimed. "You know this man? You *hired* him, you said?"

He could see the alarm in her eyes that his outburst had caused, and he immediately looked down and composed himself. Then he gave her a small smile, and got one of the other chairs so he could sit beside her.

"I'm so sorry. Please, go on."

"What did you mean, 'do I know this man'? Is his name familiar to you?"

"In a way. I'll explain in a moment. But please, Catherine, tell me what you meant that you hired him. How did you know the man?"

His use of the past tense didn't seem to surprise her, an observation of his that was verified when she answered.

"He is . . . *was* a private inquiry agent. I engaged him to investigate someone." Then she went red and looked down at the buttons on her coat. "It's an awful thing to do, I know. But I'm so concerned about Elizabeth, so worried."

"When was this?"

"Last Sunday, five days ago."

"And who did you engage him to investigate?"

"Mrs. Bain—the woman I told you about.

The weariness from lack of sleep slipped off him now and he was instantly alert.

"Tell me why you did so, Catherine. It's important. Has Mrs. Bain threatened your sister over her continuing to see Mr. Reed?"

"That's already over," replied Catherine. "Have you forgotten the letter my sister received from Ambrose on Sunday? You were there at the house. Ambrose informed Lizzie that he didn't want to see her anymore."

Yes, of course. He *had* forgotten.

"Anyway, that isn't it," Catherine went on, answering the question he'd asked previously. "I can't put my finger on anything in particular." She hesitated. "I just feel that somehow, that woman is a danger to all of us."

Scarlet was thinking furiously now. Was there a direct connection between Geach investigating Morana Bain and his awful death? Surely that was too obvious a link. London was a violent place—even West End sections like Soho, where Geach had met his end. In places like the East End and Whitechapel, it was even worse. Considering the environs Thomas Geach was surely in the habit of visiting, it wasn't far-fetched to think he had been killed while looking for Mrs. Bain, not necessarily because he was doing so.

"You say you hired this fellow five days ago," he said to Catherine now. "Had he come up with anything? Did he give you a report of any kind?"

"Only a telegram, two days ago. He wrote that he was following up on something unusual."

"Did he say anything about what that was? Did he give you a name or mention a location?"

"I'm afraid not."

She looked so miserable that he took both of her hands in his.

"You mustn't think you're responsible for this man's death in any way. You have no proof that his murder was part of the investigation he undertook for you. This was his profession, and we don't know how many clients he had. Did you read about the murder in the papers?"

She only nodded. Looking at her, he realized he'd been amiss in one respect, and kicked himself inwardly.

"How is your sister? Does she know anything of this?"

"Thank goodness, no," replied Catherine. "She is the same, which is to say, terribly unhappy. I know I shouldn't feel this way, but I'm also concerned about Ambrose. Actually, I'm worried."

When he asked what she meant, she answered: "It seems he left his house, and no one knows where he is. You see, I've . . . I've kept in touch with him, without Lizzie knowing. I'm sure that when his mind is clear, he'll realize he really loves her. It's just that this woman, this evil woman, Mrs. Bain, has turned his head. Anyway, I've sent notes to the house and they all come back, and one of the servants sent me a private note along with my returned ones, telling me that no one has seen Ambrose."

"You said 'evil' just now. Why that word in particular?"

"Oh, I don't *know*, Mr. Scarlet! But there's something about that woman—I just don't know. It's like she's . . . "

"A spider, and Ambrose is the fly?"

She smiled, despite the look of pain in her eyes. "Well, yes. That's exactly what it's like."

"Do you think that Ambrose is in trouble?"

"I wish I knew. Probably not. But he's really not well, and he should be convalescing at home."

As a physician, Scarlet agreed with that thought. Unlike Catherine, however, he knew where Ambrose was, though he didn't want to tell her and get her any more involved in this situation than she already was.

It was time to pay Ambrose Reed another visit.

CHAPTER 26

Obsession

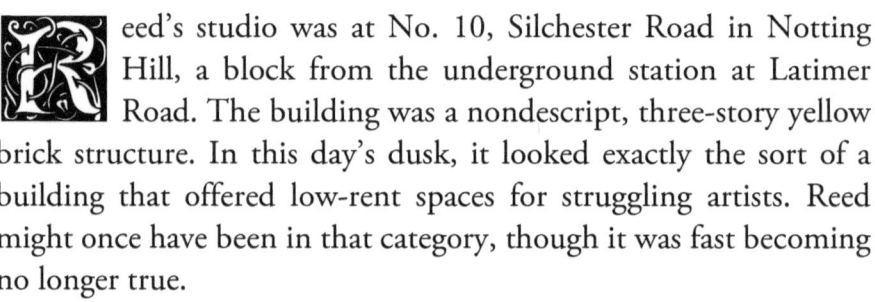eed's studio was at No. 10, Silchester Road in Notting Hill, a block from the underground station at Latimer Road. The building was a nondescript, three-story yellow brick structure. In this day's dusk, it looked exactly the sort of a building that offered low-rent spaces for struggling artists. Reed might once have been in that category, though it was fast becoming no longer true.

Scarlet and Pierce-Jones were walking fast as they entered the building. It was 6.45 p.m. on Saturday, the 15th of October, and they could only hope that the artist would be in his studio and still at work in the early evening. The two of them had been prevented from starting out earlier because Scarlet had been called down to the Yard to discuss the Geach murder. Nothing had come of the time he spent there except to set their plans back by hours.

As soon as they stepped into the building's front hall, they realized they were at a loss in yet another way. Reed hadn't given Scarlet the number of his studio, only the address. Now, in the glow of the already lit gas lamps, they could see a number of rooms on this floor; and presumably the situation was the same on the other two floors. But there was no directory with the name of each studio's occupant, as Scarlet had hoped there would be.

Though Sgt. Jessey and PC Simms had been keeping a watch

on the building, they couldn't very well have followed Reed to the door of a studio to determine which one he rented. Besides, their reports had been barren, as they hadn't seen the artist at all. That didn't necessarily mean anything, of course. Reed might have been holed up here for days already, working. That was what they had to determine this morning, one way or the other.

As they stood in the lobby pondering which studio might be Reed's, a young man emerged from one of the rooms on their right and down the hall. He had a wiry build and tousled hair, and looked every inch the artist leaving his studio after a day of work. As he approached them on his way out of the building, Pierce-Jones took a step forward. He accosted the man in an aristocratic and slightly bored voice:

"I say, we're looking for an artist by the name of Reed. Would you know which studio is his, old man?"

The other man stopped in his tracks and looked up with surprise, as though he'd been deep in thought about something.

"I'm sorry. Did you say Meade?"

"*Reed*," Django corrected him.

The look in the man's eyes changed immediately.

"Oh, yes. Ambrose Reed. Making a bit of a splash these days. I'm sure we won't see his handsome backside around here much longer. He's on the second floor, Studio C, right side. Probably there now, as he appears to have been working around the clock." He smiled. "I hope the chap is painting, and not just admiring the scenery."

Pierce-Jones shook his head, and the young man explained.

"He's engaged an extraordinary model." He thought about that characterization. "Yes, extraordinary. You'll see what I mean if they're in there working. A common girl—mill worker, that type. But a remarkable facial structure, especially the mouth and cheekbones. Quite beautiful, really."

With that thought in his mind he continued on his way, leaving Django to call out his thanks.

He walked back to Scarlet, looking self-satisfied. "Studio C, then," he said.

"Are you sure you wouldn't enjoy a spot of rowing first, *old man?*" replied his companion.

Smiling, the two men ascended the stairs.

The lights were on in three of the second-floor studios: two on the left side of the corridor and one on the right. They hoped that the lit room on the right side was Studio C.

Scarlet knocked, and they waited. No one answered and they heard no sounds in the room. He knocked again. The two of them looked at each other, and then Scarlet tried the doorknob. It twisted easily to the right. Unlocked, then. He swung the door open and they entered the studio. The place was brightly lit by gas jets from a ceiling fixture as well as a few oil lamps on tables around the room.

"Hello?" Scarlet called out, by way of announcing their presence.

Perhaps a dozen feet to their right, a man in street clothes and holding a painter's brush was sitting on a stool with his back to them, with a nearly finished canvas in front of him. Beyond the canvas, where the man seemed to be looking, was a small raised area with a model's stool on it. But there was no model sitting there. The man's hands and clothes were stained with paint, most of it a vivid blood-red. He held the brush in his right hand, which rested on that thigh. The paint on the brush appeared to be long-dried and caked onto the bristles. The man sat perfectly still. It was as though someone had created a three-dimensional image of a man sitting an at easel.

"Reed?" said Scarlet. It was obviously him, even when seen from this oblique angle.

There was no reply, and he and Pierce-Jones stepped closer, their gaze now moving to the canvas. They expected to see a young mill-girl with remarkable cheekbones. What was painted there, however, was another thing entirely.

They were looking at a portrait of a well-dressed woman in middle-age, shown down to the waist. An extraordinary cloud of dark, black, tightly-curled hair above a high forehead billowed far out on each side of the head. The face was intensely white—or *had been* white before the artist had made additions to the visage. It was a remarkably strong face, with prominent brows and arched eyebrows, a large nose, and wide lips, closed tightly. Those features gave the face a masculine look, though there was no doubt that this portrait was of a woman. She wore a white dress and black bodice with a square neckline revealing small breasts; those were skillfully depicted by Reed through subtle shadows and angles suggesting a soft rise in the fabric of the bodice. A ruby broach was pinned to the top of that garment.

All of that had been the original appearance of the picture. But the artist had then carried out a second phase of the portrait.

This had involved the red paint that now adorned both the picture and Reed's clothes. He had added gouts of blood to the woman's image, flowing from the mouth and chin downward until it covered the white neck and bosom of the subject in wide streams. Blood was smeared onto the woman's cheeks and forehead as well. Her dress too was stained by blood: rivers of it which joined as they flowed downwards until the skirts of the dress had been transformed from white to red.

Having seen all of this, the viewer's gaze inevitably returned to the face in the painting, eager, as it were, to see what the woman's response was to all this bloodletting. Was it only Scarlet's imagination that revealed a Mona Lisa-like smile on the face?

He didn't think so. He knew without a doubt now who this woman was, although he'd never met her: Morana Bain.

Where was the picture of the young model Reed was supposed to be painting? It was nowhere in the studio. Had the girl really sat for him for hours while Reed was actually busy creating this on the canvas? The thought was monstrous.

The two men now moved to before the stool, where they could see the unmoving man from the front. For a fleeting instant, Scarlet wondered if Reed was dead. He sat perfectly, stonily still—and

Scarlet realized that the artist wasn't staring at the sitting area after all, but at the painting. But it was a thousand-yard stare. Whatever he was seeing, it wasn't on the canvas in front of him.

To Scarlet and Pierce-Jones, Reed's state was more unnerving than the grotesquely bloody portrait. He was emaciated, and looked bloodless—eerily so, as though he'd given all his blood to the painting. He looked like someone who has gone without sleep for a long period, perhaps days. His lips were caked with the crust of the last bit of saliva to have moistened them; and the air around him stank with fouled breath from his not having eaten for who knew how long?

"What is this state?" asked Django.

"Catatonia," Scarlet answered. He bent down and looked at Reed more closely. "Obvious stupor, along with a profound detachment from all external stimuli. *Hoblyn's*[*] classifies it as catalepsy or loss of consciousness coupled with rigidity of the limbs. But Kahlbaum recognized it as its own psychopathological syndrome a dozen or so years ago."

He had to at least try to reach the artist, though he didn't think he was going to be successful.

"Mr. Reed?" he said. There was no reaction.

"Staring at that damnable painting would drive anyone mad," said Pierce-Jones. And then: "It's her, isn't it?"

"Mrs. Bain, you mean? Yes, I'm sure of it."

"What the devil does it mean?"

"Aside from the fact that the man is obsessed with her, I don't know."

"Why all the blood?" Pierce-Jones asked innocently.

That brought Scarlet up.

"Blood," he said, seeming to speak to himself.

"What about it?"

---

[*] Richard D. Hoblyn, A Dictionary of Terms Used in Medicine and the Collateral Sciences. Hoblyn's, as it was known, was the leading medical dictionary from its publication in 1832, to the 11th and final edition published in 1887.

Scarlet looked at his friend. "It was in my nightmare," he said, "the one I told you about. There was blood everywhere—much more than you'd see even in an operating theatre. Splashed on the walls; and actually, flowing in a tide under the doors. And in the séance, do you remember? The fountain of blood bubbling up from the table and soaking our clothes—"

"But there wasn't really any blood. It was an illusion."

"Yes, of course, that's true," said Scarlet. He was about to add, *"But we all bloody well saw it, didn't we?*, and laughed inwardly at the absurd relevance of the phrase. But he wasn't laughing when he spoke again.

"There's something about blood. I don't know what it is—but it's been part of this for me from the beginning."

"Well: surgery, autopsies, blood. It's a normal part of your world, isn't it?"

"It's more than that," Scarlet insisted. Looking again at the painting, he added: "And it was more than that for Reed as well." He shook his head and looked at his friend. "A world of blood, Django," he said, and added: "Or a case colored entirely in red."

He thought for a moment more, then dismissed the thoughts.

"Let's send word to get help for Mr. Reed here. I'm afraid he's going to need considerable care."

A half-hour later, they watched two orderlies carry a stretcher with Reed on it out of the studio. The men had instructions to take him to the psychiatric ward at St George's Hospital. Fortunately, Scarlet thought, Reed had the private resources to be housed in such a place, rather than Bethlem Royal Hospital ("Bedlam"), or the Middlesex County Lunatic Asylum at Hanwell. For a catatonic, that would be the equivalent of simply being left alone to die.

There was nothing left for them now but to leave the studio. But they didn't go. Scarlet felt instinctively that there must be something else here that would yield some kind of clue, and he knew Django well enough to sense that he felt the same. A search yielded nothing, however, except the painter's sparsely furnished workspace they had seen the moment they walked in.

And, of course, the hideous painting.

They sat on either side of it in a pair of cheap and uncomfortable wicker chairs they'd found at the back of the studio, smoking cigars and staring at the thing and thinking their own thoughts.

"Any leads on the man autopsied yesterday?" asked Pierce-Jones suddenly.

"Hm? No, nothing" replied Scarlet. His thoughts were elsewhere.

"Curious about the body's condition, though, isn't it?"

"What's that? Oh, the mutilation. Yes, certainly."

"I mean that particular type of mutilation," said Pierce-Jones.

Now Scarlet attended his friend. "You mean the delicacy of it? . . . No, that's not the word. What can one call something like that?"

But Pierce-Jones was shaking his head, and looking relaxed yet sure of himself. "You miss my point."

"I'm afraid I do," replied Scarlet.

"I mean the message that was intended."

"I don't follow."

"Well, as I say, those particular mutilations," explained Pierce-Jones. "The parts of the body the murderer targeted." He looked at his friend searchingly. "Do you mean you really don't know what I'm talking about?"

Scarlet had had enough of this banter.

"What in the devil are you getting at?"

The Roma King leaned forward, holding up his hand and counting with his fingers: "The eyes, the nose, the tongue, the ears, and the hands." He now held up five fingers. "Whoever it was cut away all of them except the ears, puncturing the eardrums instead. Don't you see, he took away all of the five senses: sight, smell, taste, hearing, and the tactile sense. He was making a statement: Geach, however good his detective skills were, would never be able to find his quarry. The task was beyond his human senses."

Scarlet sat very still for a long moment.

"Good Christ," he said.

Then he was taking long strides toward the door, shouting for Pierce-Jones to follow him.

CHAPTER 27

Gullyfluff and Shredding

he driver was pushing the horses hard, and the cab rocked and swayed like a frenzied thing. Scarlet had told him that he'd pay double the usual fare, and the man was obviously willing to strain his horses to collect it.

They had made two stops already after leaving Reed's studio, one to each of their homes to collect arms and dark lanterns*. Scarlet now carried the Metropolitan Police's new standard-issue Webley revolver in the pocket of his overcoat; while Pierce-Jones preferred the older Adams revolver. Both handguns had considerable stopping power, with calibers of .455 and .450, respectively.

They were hurrying now to their third destination of this journey. So far, the carriage's team was performing magnificently and looking good for the extra fare.

It was Saturday night in London, however, and the streets were crowded. But the driver was good, and he was using all of his skill to avoid collisions while issuing a nonstop stream of commands and invectives:

"Out of the way, you gibface!

'You, there! What makes ye think ye can drive?

---

* Editor's Note: A lantern with a panel that slides up to allow light in the forward-facing direction only, while hiding the illumination from anyone observing from behind or to the sides.

"What's that you say? . . . Why, yer a malmsey-nosed jollock. Aha!—how's that?"

Scarlet hardly heard any of it. He was thinking that this was, indeed, Saturday night—and that tomorrow night would bring the new moon. The lines of an old ballad were running in his head:

I saw the new moon late yestreen
Wi' the auld moon in her arm;
And I fear, I fear, my master dear,
I fear we'll come to harm.

They still had twenty-four hours though, more or less, if what he was thinking was true. Time enough, at least, for them to inspect the house near Battersea Park where they were headed now. Though he still knew next to nothing about Morana Bain, he knew where she lived; and they had uncovered no evidence to show that she had another place in London. When she ventured out, it would be from her home in Lurline Gardens, Battersea.

He had shared his thinking with Django while they were hailing a cab. The pieces of the mental puzzle he'd constructed weren't as clean-cut as he might have liked, but they fit.

First: *the feeling of possession of the children he'd had in his vision in Reed's bedroom*. That, coupled with the young man's obsession with Mrs. Bain . . . well, it was more than just obsession. Reed's failing health, and his loss of will pointed to some power over him that was beyond normal.

Second: *the connection with blood*. From Scarlet's nightmare, to their group hallucination in the séance, to the bloodless corpse of Thomas Geach. Also, Reed's eerie painting of Mrs. Bain, covered in blood.

Third: *Django's comment about Geach's mutilation*. The private inquiry agent had been physically deprived of his five senses, with each body part necessary for those senses carved away or punctured. Realizing that that was the message being conveyed by the carved-up corpse had crystalized Scarlet's thinking. It was as if Geach's killer were telling them loudly and clearly: *You will never find me, for it is beyond your senses to do so.*

Geach, the murdered investigator whom Catherine Wilson had hired to follow Mrs. Morana Bain.

"All roads," Scarlet thought grimly as the cab buckled and swayed, "lead to Battersea Park."

He wished that the two horses could fly.

The still-excited horses' loud snorting competed with the clammer of their hooves on the street stones as they pulled up a block from Mrs. Bain's slate-grey, three-story house. It sat as large, dark, and gloomy as any Gothic novelist would have demanded of it. That fact brought good news and not gloom, however: the darkness meant that the house was empty at the moment. Scarlet quickly handed up the promised fare to the driver and caught up to Pierce-Jones, who was walking with a determined step on the Belgian Blocks-sidewalk toward the house.

"We'll go past it at first," Scarlet whispered. "Then come back."

As they approached, they saw that the house and grounds were surrounded by a tall black iron fence. It was dark enough, Scarlet thought, to try the gate as they passed it. Whatever they planned from this point on would depend partly on whether the gate was locked or accessible.

They didn't get the chance to find out, however. As soon as they approached the gate, a fearsome barking arose inside the house, and from more than one dog. The barks, growls, and yelps from the animals were savage and eager-sounding. The two of them didn't hesitate, but left the gate and continued on their way on the sidewalk. The hellish barking continued until they were well past the house.

"That's one good thing," said Pierce-Jones, at the next corner.

"What's that?" asked the other.

"Those dogs are inside the house. They're not out on the grounds."

And leaping and thrusting their muzzles through the iron fence to rip out our throats, thought Scarlet.

"Got any magic tricks?" he asked his companion.

"I might," came the reply. "It all depends. Let's keep walking and see if the lot is large enough in the back that we can get onto the grounds without alerting those beasts."

They continued to the next corner, then turned right so that they circled the house and property on its north side. The property was sizable for a residential parcel in the center of London at around two acres, abutting an uncleared area of trees, vines, and brambles. Scattered everywhere in this thicket were exactly what one would expect to find in an untouched patch like this in the midst of a city: bits of paper and detritus, wrappers, string, an occasional bit of cast-off clothing, and corrugated paper of the type used for parcels. Surveying the thicket, Pierce-Jones gave a sound of delight.

"Now," he said, "if there's a place when the fencing has been neglected back here..."

There was. In one spot, one of the fence's vertical iron rods had fallen out—probably the result of years of jiggling by neighborhood boys to create an entrance to the grounds of what would seem to them to be a haunted house. The space was large enough for them to squeeze through one at a time. But Pierce-Jones held up a hand to stop Scarlet, who was already bending down to step through the gap.

"Don't go onto the property yet. Gather up as much of this undergrowth and gullyfluff as you can," he said.

That made Scarlet smile in the dark. Django wasn't always precisely correct in his use of English expressions. "Gullyfluff" meant the dust and other debris that collected in a schoolboy's pocket, whereas he probably meant simply garbage or trash.

"Anything dry that will crackle," he explained. "Vines, small branches, leaves, paper, and that thick material over there" (he meant some of the thick corrugated paper that lay on the ground, warped into undulating waves by the weather). "And choose some vines that are long enough to tie around a bundle."

"What are we doing," asked Scarlet, as he did as he was told. "You're not planning to smoke the dogs out, are you?"

"Something like that," said his friend enigmatically.

When they had gathered two piles of debris, Django spread each one on the ground, then knelt in front of the piles. Scarlet immediately did the same.

"This is an old Roma trick," Django said, using the everyday name for the Romani. "You start with this thick paper here, and create a box or a ball—it doesn't matter which. And you stuff it inside with these things, which really are perfect, by the way. Anything that will be tough to pull apart and that crackles and makes noise while you're trying to do that."

"Why would we want to rip apart things like this?" asked Scarlet.

"Not us, you blithering idiot—the dogs," said Django, laughing. "It's called 'shredding.' Dogs go mad for it. Apparently, it mimics the act of dissecting prey. The tougher you can make it for them to rip apart, the happier they are doing it."

"You mean, to distract these horrible beasts?"

"Exactly. This is as close as we can get in a pinch to proper shredding material. If we had more time and some good stout string, we could tie these packages properly. But we're in luck with this patch and the gullyfluff that's all around here. And the vines will be makeshift string to tie the things together."

Now that he knew what they were on about, Scarlet began the task in earnest, and they soon had four roughly-assembled shredding balls. These 'packages' also had the advantage of being easy to carry two-at-a-time because of their porous surface.

"How many dogs do you reckon are in there?" Django had asked as they'd been about the work.

"Three. Maybe four."

"I say three. Our job will be to lure them into one room and shut them inside."

"Which basically means that they'll *chase* us into that room," said Scarlet, looking unhappy at the prospect.

Pierce-Jones smiled.

"Precisely."

The two of them ducked through the fence and began approaching the house with their newly-made shredding balls and their lanterns in hand.

And that's assuming that we're right that there's no one home with a bloody great shotgun to unload on us, reflected Scarlet.

Their approach to the house didn't provoke a sound from the hellhounds. Incredibly, even the breaking of a back window by Pierce-Jones's coat-covered elbow didn't rouse them. The men now lit their dark lanterns. As Django climbed through the now-open window and placed one foot onto the floor of the house's kitchen, however, the dogs heard him and tore apart the silence with their barking.

The barking steadily increased in volume as Django lunged for the kitchen door while the dogs raced through the house to get to the kitchen first. He won the race, and slammed the door shut just in time. Instantly, the dogs were leaping up onto the door from the other side and scratching to get to the intruders inside. Scarlet, having just stepped through the open window himself, wasn't worried about any deep gouges in the wood of the door from the dogs' nails revealing their visit. Animals as savage as these would have left their marks all over the house already. Whatever breed these dogs were, it sounded like there were a dozen of them out there on the other side of the door.

Unfortunately, he couldn't think of any way he and Django would be able to get to another room in the house where the dogs could be locked in. Fortunately, Django was thinking more clearly than he was at the moment.

"This kitchen is perfect," he told Scarlet. "It's large enough for us to throw the shredding balls then stay out of the way while the dogs chase them. That should give us time to get out the door."

He picked up the two balls that he had dropped as he'd lunged to shut the dogs out. Then he gave Scarlet instructions: "You open the door, and as you do, hold it open and press yourself against the wall behind it. I'll be standing there," he indicated the other side of the door frame. "As soon as I toss the first ball, you slide around the door and make your way out of this room. The first dog will be on the ball instantly. You need to get out as soon as its attention is riveted by the ball rolling across the floor. I'll then toss the remaining three balls, and with luck the other dogs' attention will be fastened to them and I'll be able to follow you. All right?"

"And what's our back-up plan?"

"We don't have one, old man," said Pierce-Jones cheerily. "Ready?"

"Ready."

When Django was in position, Scarlet took a deep breath. He looked at his friend, who nodded sharply once. The other immediately swung the door open, at the same time stepping behind it to flatten himself against the wall.

There were only two dogs, both massive hounds. Scarlet couldn't see them yet; he could only hear the explosion of sound as they leaped inside, their barking suddenly exponentially louder. The first of the shredding balls flew across the room. As soon as Scarlet heard the dogs' nails scraping across the floor as they both bounded after it, he stepped out, caught a fleeting glance (any more than that was worth his life) at the two monsters, and was out of the kitchen, with the door open behind him.

Django told him a few minutes later what had happened next: both of the dogs reacted the same way. They hurled their huge bodies after the first shredding ball which had rolled across the kitchen floor. The hounds would have fought over it, but they were suddenly confused when *three more balls* passed them an instant later, rolling to different spots in the kitchen. They looked from one to the other of the balls, apparently unsure of which one to attack first. It gave Django enough time to follow Scarlet out of the kitchen, closing but not slamming the door behind him. The dogs didn't even attack the door from the other side, so intent were they on the round brown creatures they were now getting their revenge upon, probably to make up for the human intruders who had put them into such a frenzy.

Those intruders now began moving quickly through the house. The light from their lanterns pushed back the darkness everywhere it encountered it, keeping a narrow cone of light before them.

Nothing on the first floor drew their attention. Indeed, the furnishings were all so traditional to this type of house that it almost looked like the set of a stage play. Every piece of furniture and their arrangement was exactly right: the right designs, the right fabric, the right positioning, and of precisely the standard that would be expected of someone of Mrs. Bain's standing. They completely missed the fact that there were no mirrors anywhere, for they were intent on uncovering evidence of a different sort.

They found it on the second floor. Once they had passed through the dressing room of the master bedroom and then the bedroom itself, they discovered a small private study. Their lamps showed them a space that might have been a chapel. Indeed, that was exactly what it looked like, for it appeared to be a place of worship.

Against the wall opposite them was a long table with six tall, black candles on it. Presumably, the candles wouldn't be seen when lit from the table's position away from the only window in the room, which looked out on the back of the house. Each candle was set in a black-painted iron candlestick that wasn't straight, but curved upwards sinuously. A circle, three feet in diameter and featuring an inner and an outer ring had been painted in the center of the table. Gold letters on a black background adorned the outer ring, while inside the inner ring intricate shapes and symbols were traced in gold.

The room was dominated, however, by a large pentangle which hung on the wall behind the table. It was easily five feet in diameter, and stained a rust-red color. Scarlet knew that color, and it appalled him. To the layman, of course, blood is red. But men of science know that is due to hemoglobin, the oxygen-containing compound in iron. When blood combines with oxygen in the air, however, that iron becomes iron oxide—which is another name for rust.

He thought he knew, then, why the pentangle was of a *rust*-red color.

Otherwise, the room was sparse to the point of asceticism, except for one other item mounted on a wall, this time the wall to the left of the door. It was a large, detailed map of London, with the legend Charles Smith and Son, 1887, in the lower right corner. Scarlet and Pierce-Jones crossed to the map and looked at it closely. There were eight pins stuck into the map, each of a different color. Each pin was pressed into the paper in the exact spot where one of the children had disappeared.

Who was this woman, who presented herself to the world as the picture of propriety, but who owned such savage hounds, and who kept this room—and who presumably had placed those pins in this map?

They found nothing unusual on the rest of this floor or the third floor—only more of the picture-perfect room settings. It was time to take a look in the basement.

As they descended the stairs to the first floor, they listened for any sound from the dogs, but heard nothing. The beasts must still be enjoying their vicarious kills. Still, they moved as quietly as they could. They found the door to the basement and started down the stairs.

With fewer windows than the other parts of the house, the basement was Stygian in its gloom, and the lanterns struggled to push back the darkness. Again, they saw nothing noteworthy at first glance. But they had discussed earlier what they might find here, and now they moved directly to the object they were looking for.

The coal-fired furnace they found was bigger than they had expected, even in a home of this size. A large square of metal was bolted onto the front with the legend HEAVY DUTY BOILER

PLATE. Below that, the door to the combustion chamber was embossed with the brand name MAJESTIC. Scarlet grasped the handle, its black paint worn away from years of use so that the handle was white, and opened the door. The two of them bent down and peered in.

They saw piles of bones—the largest bones white, the longer, thinner ones black. Scarlet knew that bones located in the center of the human body will burn hotter in a furnace due to the presence of fat, so that they became pure white. The bones of limbs, on the other hand, will only burn to black. What they were looking at, then, were the white bones of torsos, and the blackened bones of arms and legs. They were all human, and all were the size of children's bones.

Scarlet closed the furnace door and neither of them spoke for a moment. Then he looked at Pierce-Jones and said sharply:

"How many children have disappeared?"

"Seven."

"And how many pins are there in the map upstairs?"

Django's eyes widened slightly, then he said: "Eight."

They took the flights of stairs to the second floor two at a time and were quickly back in the inner room and the map. The eighth pin—a red one—was pressed into the area near the southeastern tip of Hyde Park.

Pierce-Jones was the first to speak.

"This will be the location of this woman's next victim, then?"

"I can come to no other conclusion," answered Scarlet. "And it must be tomorrow night—the night of the new moon."

"But I don't understand," said Django. "This is a public park. It's not a slum or a rookery, or even an alley."

"Not all the children's abductions were in neighborhoods like that."

"But Hyde Park is famous. It's bound to be filled with people."

"Not in the dark of night, especially with a new moon," Scarlet replied. "Still, you're right: it's puzzling. Why here? There must be some reason." He leaned in to look at the map more closely, as if there were something printed on the image that had been too small to see previously. But there was nothing. He said to himself: "What's there?"

Then his frown disappeared, and he nodded and said: "That's it!" He looked at Django as if to say, "Can't you see it?" and he *did* say: "The Boy and Dolphin Fountain. That's right where this pin is set. Children flock to it. What could be more certain to attract them to the park?"

Pierce-Jones's face was grim as he answered.

"Where she'll be waiting for them."

But Scarlet wasn't buying into that mood.

"Come on," he said, sounding excited. "We have much to do before tomorrow night!"

CHAPTER 28

Demon in View

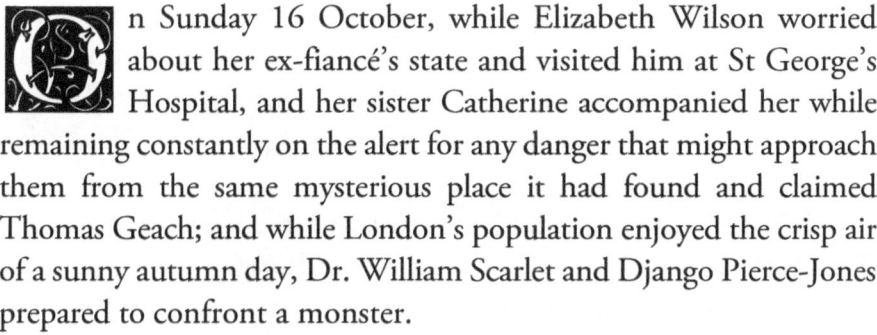n Sunday 16 October, while Elizabeth Wilson worried about her ex-fiancé's state and visited him at St George's Hospital, and her sister Catherine accompanied her while remaining constantly on the alert for any danger that might approach them from the same mysterious place it had found and claimed Thomas Geach; and while London's population enjoyed the crisp air of a sunny autumn day, Dr. William Scarlet and Django Pierce-Jones prepared to confront a monster.

Whether the revolvers they now carried would be helpful was a question they couldn't answer. Any other weapons or tools which might help them also remained unknown to them, for they didn't know the power of their enemy. Even the question of *who* or *what* they were facing wasn't a simple matter.

At least they had time, for both of them were certain nothing would happen until tonight's new moon. The recurrence of the lunar cycle that had played out in the other children's disappearances—and as they believed they now knew, their murders—seemed to be a set pattern for the perpetrator. But time was also a dilemma for them. An almanac had informed them that the new moon would rise tonight at 10.33. What children would be visiting even a famous children's statue that late at night, in a dark public park?

At any rate, they would not be alone in their surveillance of the area. Scotland Yard was already out in force, given the link between the earlier disappearances and the new moon. Scarlet had advised Mallinson—with as much circumspection as he could manage—that constables should be stationed near the Boy and Dolphin Fountain in Hyde Park. It was as much as he dared to do, as he still couldn't share with his superior the séance and the evidence that had emerged from it. Fortunately, policemen would already be in the London parks, on alert, from dusk onward. Directing them to keep a special eye out in the area of the fountain would only be a slight re-direction of the Yard's strategy.

But the Metropolitan Police would also be spread dangerously thin tonight. The city encompassed nearly 700 square miles, with a population of five-and-a-half millions—ten times the land area of New York City and twice its population. If Scarlet was wrong about the location of tonight's danger—and doubly wrong if Mrs. Bain was not the right suspect—the city represented a gigantic killing field they could not possibly cover.

It also promised to be a long night with the new moon rising so late. Scarlet and Pierce-Jones both took advantage of the Sunday, therefore, to take a nap in the afternoon so they could be fresh and ready when the sun went down.

They met at the fountain at 4.00 p.m. Pierce-Jones was already there when Scarlet arrived.

"About time," Pierce-Jones scolded. His tone was light and teasing, however. Scarlet thought The Roma King was trying to make their rendezvous appear ordinary.

"Rubbish," said Scarlet. "I'm right on time."

"Well, a few minutes later and you may not have found me here," Django protested. "A Peeler was ready to arrest me. Questioned me closely as to why I was spending so much time around the children's fountain."

"It's that dark exotic look and those curls of yours," his friend replied. "He probably just wanted to chat you up to go to the dance hall with him and needed a way to strike up a conversation."

Then he became serious.

"An hour to dusk?"

"Precisely," Django replied.

Sundown would be at 5.06 today—and that time might be important. Sarah Gates—the only child sighted just prior to a disappearance—had been seen walking with a stranger in the late dusk on the 20th of July, so that time of day was a possibility for any new abductions. But the other children had disappeared in the late evening or at night, which increased the odds of a later taking.

There was another sobering thought: tonight was the first night of the new moon. That phase would last for a second night as well. What if the killer wouldn't be out tonight at all, but was planning to strike tomorrow night, the 17th?

Two long nights of heightened tension for hours on end didn't appeal to either of them. They hadn't discussed that possibility except in passing last night. But it was something they might have to deal with. Scarlet found himself hoping that whatever happened during this new moon, would take place tonight.

Looking around him, he felt a new confidence that they were in the right place. The fountain plaza was circular, with four paths leading to it from different parts of the park. The fountain itself rose from its own circle of paving stones. Above the two-tiered base was a large round basin to collect the water. Set in the basin was a stone of unfinished granite, and atop the stone crouched the boy, with his right arm clutching the head scales and his left arm grasping the tale of a rather grotesque-looking dolphin.

Four paths, then, with heavy shrubbery and benches in the spaces between them. Four directions an attacker might come from, with abundant foliage to conceal him or her until the last moment. Equally bad, the foliage was mostly evergreen, which meant it hadn't lost its leaves even though it was now mid-October. It was a surveillance team's nightmare.

And an ideal spot for the abductor-and-murderer to have chosen.

It was late enough in the day now that the area wasn't crowded, even on what had been a sunny afternoon. An equal number of families and governesses pushing prams made a beeline for the fountain as they arrived via one of the paths, staying there long enough for their charges to get their fill. The children were all delighted with the fountain which bubbled merrily, while their parents or guardians were mostly patiently stoic, looking like they were anxious to get home.

An hour later, everyone was gone—and Scarlet was impressed with how even a popular location gives way at the end of the day to abandonment and stillness. That thought quickly gave way, however, to self-admonishment and a reminder that he'd better stop playing philosopher and keep his mind sharp.

Dusk gave way to evening, evening to night. A naked boy cavorted with a monstrous dolphin, and whether there was anyone apart from police constables waiting nearby in the darkness, he couldn't tell. He had situated himself behind an overgrown bush on one of the paths leading to the fountain, while Django was hidden in a stand of trees across the circle from him.

The air was cool now, not cold, but Scarlet wasn't dressed for it. He remembered what someone had told him once: that we feel coldest not on winter days, but when we're outside for long periods in the mid- to late-fall, and we're dressed just a bit too thinly for the temperature. That was exactly how he felt now.

Worse, was the fact that they were waiting for a new moon to rise above the earth. They were in the wrong place to see the part of the horizon where it would become visible.

They waited. One hundred years seemed to have passed since they began their surveillance.

Now he heard voices on the path directly behind him.

Children's voices.

There were at least two voices, from boys ten- or eleven-years old speaking in the language of the working class. They seemed to be ragging someone else who was with them—by the sound of it, a younger boy.

"No y'don't, Willum! Get back 'ere. We come all this way 'cause you wanted to."

"That's the truth of it, Willie," agreed a second lad. "Yer the one that wanted to see the bleedin' statue." This one's voice became younger and whiny: "I want 'er see it! I want 'er see it! The boy and the dolphink!"

The two boys who had spoken laughed.

The three of them came into view now, emerging from the path just to Scarlet's right. There were two boys of the age he guessed, pulling a lad of five or six behind them by his coat collar. They were dressed shabbily. The two older boys appeared to be enjoying themselves, despite their criticism of the younger lad.

"We exscaped through the cellar to come 'ere, and now we's 'ere," said the first boy. Scarlet could see he was the oldest of the three, and from his resemblance to the younger child, was probably his brother. "Better do as we say, or we leave you here, Willum."

They had stopped now, halfway between the end of the path and the circle of cobblestones in front of the fountain. They'd be able to see it well enough from there. But it was obvious that the darkness and the strange surroundings had scared the little boy. He couldn't prevent his brother and the other boy from pulling him forward, but Scarlet could hear him start to sniffle. Another moment and he'd be crying outright.

Then the temperature suddenly became much colder. It was palpable, and uncanny—as if a patch of Arctic air had descended upon them. Scarlet's gaze was still focused on the boys, and he saw the older two look at each other. Did it also become darker? It was hard to say. No, *something* was darker than it had been before: a vertical patch of blackness that he could see against the background of the trees directly opposite him—the same section of trees where Django was hidden. The black place appeared to be human in shape and height . . . or was he just imagining it? He wasn't, for he saw it separate itself from the background of foliage and begin to move forward, toward the fountain.

The second boy said, his voice frightened now: "Um, Dick . . . we can let Willie go home now, can't—"

"RUN!" shouted the other.

The two older boys took off like a shot, sprinting for the path they had come in by and were quickly out of sight. But little William was frozen. He stood stock-still, watching the moving darkness approach him.

Incomprehension froze Scarlet for a few seconds, but no more than that. With a quick look across the fountain—long enough to see Django crashing out of the tree-line—he started across the distance between him and the boy. It was no more than a dozen feet, and his thigh muscles propelled him quickly from stillness to a full run. But halfway there, he stopped short, breathing hard and staring at the scene in front of him.

Time must have warped into something unrecognizable—for things couldn't have happened so fast. A woman stood where no one had been an instant before, with William cradled in her arms. The boy's head lolled backward at a severe angle where the woman's arms didn't support him, the white flesh of his face and neck starkly visible. The woman and Scarlet stood still, looking into the face of the other.

It was the woman he'd seen in the portrait at Reed's studio. The distinctive billow of dark hair, the deep brows, the prominent nose, and the wide mouth and strong chin—all told him this was Morana Bain. But it was a Mrs. Bain now transformed into something else. The face was exceptionally pale; the eyes glowed with an unearthly light, while fingers as curled as talons held little William. The silence was deep enough that Scarlet could hear the boy's steady, slow breathing. The mouth of the woman—the thing—turned upward into a hard smile. Even without moonlight Scarlet could see the hard sharp teeth.

Then, still smiling, she opened her arms. The boy, without anything to break the fall, fell onto the hard paving stones with a dull thud.

Again, time seemed to flicker. Scarlet was now looking down at the boy, unconscious on the paving stones. The woman was gone. His gaze rose and he saw Pierce-Jones standing on the other side of the prostrate lad, looking down at him. One or both of them must have yelled something when they broke out of their hiding places, for police constables were converging now on the fountain from all four of the paths. Then Scarlet was able to move again and he bent down for a quick examination of the lad. He saw no marks or injuries of any kind.

"Where did she go?" he asked, standing. It was a ludicrous question, but it came out without him thinking about it.

Django shook his head. His shocked face, Scarlet knew, was a mirror of his own. The woman, or whatever she was, had vanished as completely as if she'd never existed.

Now two constables were carrying the boy, on their way to hospital. Scarlet and Pierce-Jones were talking with the other policemen, about what each of them had seen and heard. The discussion was about a suspicious woman's attempt to kidnap the boy, and Scarlet left it at that. He gave them the names of William and Richard, or 'Dick.' With the help of some canvassing of neighborhoods, he was sure that Willum would be safely back with his family before dawn.

Pierce-Jones was visibly relieved. But Scarlet looked serious, thinking intently about something. Normally, Django would leave him to his thoughts at moments like this. But his relief was overwhelming and he needed to give voice to it.

"Thank Heavens we guessed right," he said. "The boy is safe, and it won't be long before we run that . . . thing down to earth."

Scarlet glanced at him, as if to show that he'd heard what Django had said but couldn't respond right now. Part of his mind recognized that The Roma King, a medium, had readily accepted that they were dealing with more than an evil woman—that in fact the Other Side was involved in this horrible drama. He was glad that that thought wasn't his alone.

He began to walk back and forth, a few steps each away. He looked ready for action, but unsure of how he should initiate it.

"You don't understand," he said to his friend.

"What do you mean?"

"I mean, this isn't the end of it. This isn't this woman's endgame." It was easier to call her that than anything else at the moment.

Pierce-Jones was frowning.

"But we know each of the abductions, and the subsequent murders, occurred on the nights of the new moon. That's tonight. And the map—"

"Yes, of course," said Scarlet impatiently. "But it's a means to an end for Mrs. Bain, or whatever name we should call her. Don't you see, it's Reed that matters? And seeing what he's going through . . ." He broke off, obviously thinking hard again.

"You're right," declared Django. "I don't understand."

Now Scarlet began thinking out loud, unaware, or perhaps unconcerned, that he wasn't making sense yet in the mind of his friend.

"I can't help feeling that it will happen soon. But of course, I don't know when, because I can't tell whether Reed is ready yet. I don't know the signs to look for—or whether we've seen them already. Or even where . . ."

He stopped and looked sharply around him. He asked, his voice urgent: "How far is St George's Hospital from here?"

"Not far," answered Django. Two-tenths of a mile?"

"Yes, that's just about right," Scarlet agreed, for his question had been more in the way of seeking confirmation. "What a bloody fool!" he added, and began running up one of the paths. "Come on!" he yelled.

"Where?" Pierce-Jones shouted back, sounding equally baffled and confounded. "What's going on?"

"A bloody fool!" Scarlet said again, as he disappeared rapidly up the path.

CHAPTER 29

The Screaming Demon

e suddenly realized that there were no constables following them. Somehow, they mustn't have noticed him and Pierce-Jones running from the park.

Doesn't matter. They won't be any help. Odd they didn't see us, though.

He was sprinting now, his thoughts as random as the wind, blowing one way then another. His hat had blown off, and he heard himself struggling to get lungsful of air as he ran. Django's breathing, just like his, was right behind him.

He hardly looked out for any cabs on the carriage drive and then Knightsbridge as they sprinted out of the park and across both roadways. Another stretch of grass, and then there was St George's Hospital. The building rose, solid and stalwart, its painted stucco exterior almost dazzlingly white, even at night. There—the familiar Doric columns, heralds to the institution's stateliness, and the two massive wings standing like guardians on either side of the central structure.

And the Union Jack, fluttering in the night sky high above the pitched roof. Surely, nothing evil could infiltrate this proud symbol of nineteenth-century rationalism and science.

But Scarlet was afraid that something already had.

As they approached the main entrance, he knew it was useless to ask if anyone had noticed a woman walking past the front desk, perhaps twenty minutes before. Twenty minutes! Django and he had wasted that much time chatting with the policemen! He should have guessed the significance of the proximity of the fountain to St George's, as soon as he'd seen the pins on the map of London. They should have headed straight for the hospital once the boy was safe! Now, he could only hope that they weren't too late.

The other feeling gnawing at his gut was just as bad: He wasn't sure what they could do, even if they were in time.

Scarlet knew the layout of St George's as well as he knew any building in the world. So, he didn't stop at the front desk or pay attention to anyone in the corridors who might have stopped them. Fortunately, the staff on duty recognized him, and didn't seem concerned that he and a companion were arriving this late at night. Still, he slowed down to a fast walk as he made his way past the desk, knowing that behind him Django would be doing the same. No need to raise a general alarm by sprinting past everyone and raising a crowd of followers.

But as soon as they had made their way through the entrance hall and past the rotunda, they began running at full speed down the main corridor. They sprinted up the stairs to the second floor. The psychiatric ward was located near the end of the eastern wing of the building. Beyond the ward was a suite of private rooms, and Scarlet knew that Reed had been placed in one of them. Again, they resumed a walking pace as they passed through the ward so as not to awaken anyone.

The room they wanted was the one directly in front of them as they emerged from the ward. It was the last room at the end of the wing, its entrance facing the ward. Even if Scarlet had not known that this was Reed's room, the red glow emanating from it would have told him that this was the place he wanted.

He and Django stopped, watching the eerie, flickering red light reflected on the ceiling of the corridor, listening for any sounds coming from the room. But there were none. Both of them drew their revolvers from their coats and fanned out to either side of the door, weapons at the ready. Then with a synchronized nod, they stepped into the room—but one step only, ready to back up into the corridor if they needed to.

If there were such a thing as Hell on earth, Scarlet thought, he was seeing it now. The scene before them was like a ritual being acted out: some ancient rite performed in the glowing red light of a volcano. Where the light came from he couldn't tell, but hellish was the right word for it. It turned every shadow—including those on faces—from gray to black.

There were four figures in the room. Reed was in the bed, lying on his back with his eyes closed. Standing next to the bed to his right was Mrs. Bain, with her arms extended and the palms of both hands placed on his chest. Two women were standing in mid-motion, frozen into stillness halfway between the bed and a pair of chairs against the wall. The light in the room was so eerie that it took Scarlet a moment to recognize Elizabeth and Catherine Wilson.

Painted hurriedly on the wall behind Reed's head was the same pentangle-in-a-circle they had seen in Morana Bain's house. Its color was the same rust-red that it had been in that version of the symbol. From this freshly painted one, however, rivulets ran down the wall.

Good, thought Scarlet: *That's old blood, not new.*

He realized that Mrs. Bain was speaking, reciting something softly. She was incanting unfamiliar words in nearly a whisper. Whether she knew that he and Django were in the room now wasn't certain; her eyes were closed as she recited the incantation. Suddenly, as had happened at the fountain, the air in the room turned frigid.

A small black spot appeared in the center of the pentangle on the wall and immediately began to expand. In less than thirty seconds, it grew big enough to blot out the circle. It continued to expand until the entire wall behind the bed was an impenetrable black region that somehow seemed to have depth.

Scarlet felt as frozen as the two women. It was impossible to know what to do. Mrs. Bain's hands, that had been laid flat on Reed's hospital gown, suddenly grasped the fabric and pulled him up into a sitting position. Then, with hideous strength, she lifted him completely out of the bed until he stood, the tips of his toes on the floor and his body arched upward, as the powerful thing beside the bed held him up by the top of his gown.

In a single stride, Mrs. Bain stepped into the wall of blackness—*and at once her left leg, arm, and shoulder were no longer visible!* Only her head and the right half of her was still in the room, encumbered by the unconscious young man she was now dragging behind her. But her movement abruptly stopped, as though she were unable to go any deeper into that darkness.

Then, all hell broke loose.

A deep roaring sound arose and grew until it blocked out every thought in Scarlet's mind. It seemed to come from the veil of darkness that had once been the wall behind the bed. Then he realized he could hear other sounds. Somewhere, a woman was yelling something . . . but her voice wasn't close enough for him to understand what she was saying. Another voice screamed back at the woman—a harsh, inhuman voice. That one was female, too. The voice was filled with hatred, but the words were in some language Scarlet didn't understand. There! A man's voice now, pleading with the harsh voice—they spoke back and forth for a moment. . . . *Was it Reed's voice?* Now the roaring noise had changed to a fiercely howling wind, like a storm at the edge of the world.

A huge snake—at least eight feet long and perhaps two feet in diameter—was slithering on the floor, making its way rapidly around everyone's feet. Scarlet recognized it as the same one that had appeared in the séance. Just as he had the thought, the same voice cried out as it had then:

KILL THE SERPENT!

Now everyone was in motion:

Pierce-Jones was aiming his revolver at the snake.

The two women were able to move again. Elizabeth Wilson was rounding the bed to where Reed lay on the floor, being half-dragged toward the blackness.

Her sister Catherine was grasping Scarlet's right arm.

He shook her off roughly, lunging forward and deflecting Django's hand downward before he could fire. Then, with a desperate lunge which threw him on the floor, he grabbed hold of Reed's left leg with both of his hands.

Mrs. Bain was trying to step deeper into the wall—or whatever in God's name that black place was now. But she was struggling, unable to do so. Scarlet thought at first that it was his resistance that was impeding her, as he held onto Reed and pulled the young man as hard as he could in his own direction. But only a few seconds later, he understood that that wasn't the case.

Somebody else was suddenly visible, standing on the other side of the bed. A small woman with tight dark curls, wearing a white shroud and an emerald necklace. The woman's gaze was riveted on Mrs. Bain, a terrible look in her eyes. Mrs. Bain turned toward her and for a moment, her eyes were locked with those of the younger, smaller woman. Then the older woman turned back to the blackness, and made one last attempt to push her way into the wall.

She seemed to heave but without success, then her head snapped backward. Abruptly, she faded from view; was visible again; faded once more. A piercing scream suddenly rose high above the sound of the wind: unearthly and inhuman. It was like the cumulative scream of eons—a desperate agonized mix of hatred, fear, and failure. Morana Bain faded one last time . . . and this time, did not come back. The scream continued to ride the night air like something demonic. Then it began slowly to diminish, until it faded away completely.

Then they were in a private room in St George's Hospital: five people looking at each other, for Reed was awake and staring up at the others from the floor beside Scarlet. No one spoke. The atmosphere in the room was like the aftermath of a storm. Everything was quiet and still, with the stillness that follows a cataclysm that has just passed through a place.

CHAPTER 30

The Unbreakable Vow

Saturday 22 October. Nine Columns, Beatrice Road, London, N4.

illiam Scarlet looked across the Wilsons' drawing room at Ambrose Reed, thinking how relatively healthy the young artist looked. It had been six days since the horror in the private room at St George's Hospital. Reed still looked frail, and it would be another two or three weeks before he recovered fully. But his color was good, and that was an excellent sign.

Elizabeth Wilson was sitting on the arm rest of Ambrose's chair, her left arm draped around him and every so often patting his shoulder with her hand. Despite whoever was speaking at any moment, her gaze was almost always to be found centered on her fiancé. The late-morning light from the windows bathed Reed's face, which had a peaceful look, like Lazarus relishing the light of day again. Scarlet had a momentary vision of the black, swallowing wall in the hospital room, and banished it with a small shudder he hoped no one saw.

He sat at one end of the room's couch. Catherine Wilson occupied the other end. Django Pierce-Jones had sole possession of the powder-blue armchair nearest the window, looking wonderfully exotic and out-of-place. To Scarlet's mind, the entire scene—the beautifully designed and painted drawing room, the languid morning, the social chit-chat of the privileged class, the discrete separation of the sexes (except for the betrothed couple)—seemed so proper and wildly different from the last experience this group had been through together that it was hardly believable.

He smiled to himself, relishing every second of this time and place.

"So, we'll never know," said Caroline Wilson, setting down her tea cup and picking up on their discussion from a moment ago.

There was a momentary silence.

"Whether Morana Bain was really something evil?" Scarlet responded.

"No. Of course, she was. I mean, whether she was, well, what you'd call a demon. Or something like that," she added, apparently feeling the need to soften the outrageous statement.

"I think you're really asking whether I think demons exist," said Scarlet, "who have powers which none of us can understand. I believe the answer to that is yes, and that Morana Bain was one of them. To do what she did, and to have the abilities she exhibited in that hospital room . . . " He let the thought trail off.

"Thank goodness we had the power to defeat her," said Catherine.

"Well, it was the unbreakable vow, wasn't it?"

Everyone looked at Elizabeth Wilson, as no one had expected her to join the discussion. They had thought all of her attention was on Reed.

She explained.

"It was Mary Reed, Ambrose's first wife." Her gaze fell on her fiancé, and she went on looking at him. "I don't believe it was a hallucination at all. Mary knew what Morana Bain was. That's why she stopped her from taking Ambrose."

"And what is the unbreakable vow?" asked Pierce-Jones.

"Her marriage vow," answered Elizabeth. "She simply didn't allow the 'till death do us part' language to intervene. She was an incredible woman, and she proved to us that there's something after death. That was her we saw beside the bed. Wasn't it, Ambrose?"

It was the question no one had wanted to ask him until now, waiting for the day when he was strong enough to hear it.

Reed nodded, but looked downward, evidently dwelling in his own thoughts. Then he said, still staring at the blue rug that occupied the center of the drawing room:

"Your mother was wrong, Lizzie. Mary wasn't trying to disrupt our engagement and keep me from marrying again. She was trying to protect me all along, even from beyond the grave."

Scarlet agreed with that assessment. Only he knew how wrong he'd been initially in suspecting Reed and his deceased wife in the children's disappearance.

He said now:

"That explains what happened in our séance. The appearance of the snake—probably Morana's familiar—and the words we heard shouted, 'Kill the serpent!' Then your name, shouted twice. That was all Mary, fighting Mrs. Bain even then."

Reed considered that for a long moment. Then he said quietly: "She loved me, after all."

"Of course, she did, darling," said Elizabeth, and bent to kiss him.

"So did Mrs. Bain," added Catherine, with the look of a woman who prefers reality to sentiment.

Reed laughed uncertainly, and Pierce-Jones added:

"She was a demon in love."

"Which is why she was trying to take you to The Other Side," added Scarlet. Though the truth was horrible, it was good to get all of it out now, so Reed wouldn't have lingering doubts. "That was her plan all along. She had already been feeding on you psychically for some time, making you weaker and weaker until the time came when she was able to take you over completely."

"Thank God, you got there in time," said Reed.

Scarlet shook his head. "Again, not us—Mary."

"Was she able to destroy Mrs. Bain?" asked Elizabeth.

"Probably not," said Scarlet. "But at least, to banish her from this side of the veil, and prevent the terrible thing she was trying to accomplish. My theory—and it's just a theory—is that only someone in the afterlife who has already passed over has the power to fight someone on The Other Side.

"That's what ultimately destroyed Mrs. Bain, incidentally—or the demon that she really was. She wasn't powerful enough to manifest herself here as Morana Bain, a human being, while retaining her full power on The Other Side. If she had come over completely, she'd have had to temporarily give up her power in the afterlife. She had to maintain a presence on both sides of the veil to carry out her plan. But to do that she needed to feed her human manifestation, because she didn't have enough strength to survive here on her own."

To the confused looks which met Scarlet's explanation, Pierce-Jones added:

"Hence, the children's murders."

After a moment's pause, Elizabeth Wilson said, in a soft voice:

"She was feeding on them."

"Yes," said Scarlet. "And this time, physically. She mustn't have been strong enough to attack adult humans. So, it had to be children. She incapacitated them somehow and took them back to her house. There, she fed on their life source—undoubtedly by taking their blood. And then disposing of their bodies in the furnace."

"But what about Mr. Geach?" asked Catherine, looking like she regretted having hired the man at all. "Didn't she feed on him? You said there was a puncture of some sort in his leg vein that allowed the blood to be removed quickly."

"The femoral artery, not a vein," said Scarlet.

He shook his head.

"All those vampire stories from Eastern Europe get it wrong, you see. Vampires are always attaching themselves to their victims' necks—to the carotid artery. But the femoral arteries in the legs have a greater blood pressure and volume than the carotids. They're much more efficient for anyone wanting to empty a body of its blood quickly." He smiled grimly. "I suppose the vampires in their coffins simply don't have the time to go to medical school."

But Catherine persisted. "You can joke if you want, sir. But Morana Bain *did* kill Mr. Geach, didn't she? If so, she apparently had the strength in that instance to feed on him."

"No—that was a simple murder," Scarlet replied. "Geach must have been getting too close to Mrs. Bain's secret. So, she eliminated him. Then the demon that she is couldn't resist mutilating Geach by taking away his five senses, cutting out parts of his body and puncturing the eardrums. She—*it*—was telling us: 'You'll never find me using your human senses.' It was part of the demon's arrogance, I'd venture.

"As to overpowering him, she must have used some instrument to puncture the femoral artery quickly. That would not only make Geach's blood pressure plummet suddenly so he became incapacitated, but it was also the reason no blood was found at the scene. I think that if you go to the alley where he was found, you'll discover a grate somewhere close by leading to a sewer drain."

Catherine accepted this explanation with a slight nod. But her sister was clearly disturbed.

"It's too awful," ventured Elizabeth. "Those poor people. . . . Dr. Scarlet, what will Scotland Yard's official verdict be concerning Mr. Geach's murder and that of the children?"

"A coroner's verdict will be entered individually in each of the cases. And I'm afraid each verdict will remain the same as it has been up to now: 'Unlawful killing by person or persons unknown.'"

"Well," added Catherine Wilson, ever the realist: "You can't very well claim that a demon committed the murders and have anyone believe it, can you?"

They all thought about that for a moment.

Only later would Scarlet speak with Pierce-Jones about the unexpected upshot of all of this: that the strange events of a demon in love were destined to be the first recorded case of The Society for Supernatural and Psychic Research.

But let that come in the near future. Now, a sunny late-October morning and friends were waiting.

"Is there any more tea?" asked William Scarlet.

If you liked *Red Season*, please consider contributing a review on Amazon or wherever you bought the book!

Ready to follow Dr. Scarlet and Django Pierce-Jones as they investigate their next case?

Keep reading for an excerpt from *Year of the Rippers* — Book 2 in the Dr. William Scarlet Mysteries.

PROLOGUE

The Second Murder

DIVISIONAL REFERENCE H302

Submitted through Ex: Bch: H Division

Commercial Street 30o/1
METROPOLITAN POLICE.
H Division.
8th September 1888

I beg to report that at 6.10 a.m. 8th inst. while on duty in Commercial Street, Spitalfields, I received information that a woman had been murdered. I at once proceeded to No. 29 Hanbury Street, and in the back yard found a woman lying on her back, dead, left arm resting on left breast, legs drawn up, abducted small intestines and flap of the abdomen lying on right side, above right shoulder attached by a cord with the rest of the intestines inside the body; two flap of skin from the lower part of the abdomen lying in a large quantity of blood above the left shoulder; throat cut deeply from left and back in a jagged manner right around throat. I at once sent for Dr. Phillips Div. Surgeon and to the Station for the ambulance and assistance. The Doctor pronounced life extinct and stated the woman had been dead at least two hours. The body was then removed on the Police ambulance to the Whitechapel mortuary.

On examining the yard I found on the back wall of the house (at the head of the body) and about 18 inches from the ground about 6 patches of blood varying in size from a sixpenny piece to a point, and on the wooden pailing on left of the body near the head patches and smears of blood about 14 inches from the ground.

The woman has been identified by Timothy Donovan "Deputy" Crossinghams Lodging house 35 Dorset Street, Spitalfields, who states he has known her about 16 months, as a prostitute and for the past 4 months she had lodged at above house and at 1.45 a.m. 8th inst. she was in the kitchen, the worse for liquor and eating potatoes, he Donovan sent to her for the money for her bed, which she said she had not got and asked him to trust her which he declined to do she then left stating that she would not be long gone; he saw no man in her company.

Description, Annie Siffey age 45, length 5 ft, complexion fair, hair (wavy) dark brown, eyes blue, two teeth deficient in lower jaw, large thick nose; dress black figured jacket, brown bodice, black skirt, lace boots, all old and dirty.

A description of the woman has been circulated by wire to All Stations and a special enquiry called for at Lodging Houses &c to ascertain if any men of a suspicious character or having blood on their clothing entered after 2 am 8th inst.

JL.Chandler Inspr.

Annie Chapman—sometimes known as "Siffey," "Sivvey," or "Sievey" because she had lived with a man who was a sieve maker—was found murdered two days after the funeral of Mary Ann Nichols, slain eight days earlier. The awful possibility that a crazed killer was stalking London's East End seemed to have been confirmed.

Three more murders like this one would follow over the next three months, before the toll of women slaughtered and mutilated by a shadowy killer finally ended in November. Or so it seemed. In reality, there would be *seven* more killings—though the world would never connect four of them with the soon-to-become famous murderer of London prostitutes in Whitechapel and Spitalfields.

Most curious of all, the monster known as "Jack the Ripper" would have nothing to do with any of these killings.

The narrative that follows concerns what actually happened in London in the summer and fall of The Year of Our Lord eighteen hundred and eighty-eight. It is the true story of that awful time, told at last.

CHAPTER 1

Doss Houses and Phossy Jaw

Whitechapel is a section of London's East End, though to its residents in the year 1888 it may have seemed more like the world's end. It was a place of desperate poverty and a constant struggle to survive. To the fur pullers who cleaned rabbit skins for a living and worked in enclosed places filled with fluff and hair, it was a struggle just to breathe. To the masses who overburdened the labor market in the area, it was a never-ending struggle to find work. To the girls who worked in the match factories, it was a doomed effort to avoid "phossy jaw," in which the phosphorous from the matches ate away their jaws and then killed them. To the fallen women forced to walk the streets for immoral purposes after midnight, lifting their skirts while braced against a grimy brick wall—London's "unfortunates"—it was a struggle to gain the few pence necessary to secure a bed for the night.

The doss houses, or common lodging places, were waiting for them when they succeeded.

A doss house would provide you with a bed in an overcrowded dormitory for four pence a night, and where you could use the central kitchen to cook whatever you were able to scrounge or steal that day. For low-wage working men, prostitutes, and anyone desperately down on their luck, it offered a place to spend the night that was one step up from the street.

In Whitechapel alone in the year of our story, out of a population of about a quarter million, the Metropolitan Police estimated that there were 1,200 prostitutes, and over 60 brothels. There were 149 registered doss houses or "hostels," and an unknown number of unregistered ones.

In the docks area of St George in the East, the poverty rate was nearly 49 percent. And the mortality rate in the poor quarters of England's cities was such that one of every five children didn't make it past their first year.

It was in this world of misery and desperation—where lived the People of the Abyss—that the murders began.

GARY GENARD is the author of the Dr. William Scarlet mysteries. He lives in Massachusetts. You can find his fiction and nonfiction books at www.garygenard.com.

www.ingramcontent.com/pod-product-compliance
Lightning Source LLC
LaVergne TN
LVHW041632060526
838200LV00040B/1549